STILLE! UNTOTEN!

RAUS! UNTOTEN! VOLUME TWO

EDITED BY MATTHEW SYLVESTER

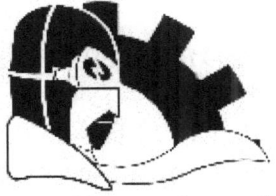

www.fringeworks.co.uk

Edited by Matthew Sylvester
Cover by Jason Zerrillo

"Foreword" © Matthew Sylvester
"Les Foupe's Gris" © Nas Hedron
"Love is Stronger" © Stewart Hotston
"Pulse" © Ian Hall
"Rise of the Secret King" © Gav Thorpe
"Eternal Reich" © Jamie Mason
"Red was the Night" © Alex Helm

Copyright © 2014, Fringeworks Ltd
First published in Great Britain in 2014 by
FRINGEWORKS LTD
www.fringeworks.co.uk

ISBN: 978-1-909573-21-5

CONTENTS

FOREWORD
BY MATTHEW SLYVESTER_____1

LES POUPE'S GRIS
BY NAS HEDRON_____5

LOVE IS STRONGER
BY STEWART HOTSTON_____27

PULSE
BY IAN HALL_____39

RISE OF THE SECRET KING
BY GAV THORPE_____57

ETERNAL REICH
BY JAMIE MASON_____79

RED WAS THE NIGHT
BY ALEX HELM_____93

FOREWORD

BY MATTHEW SLYVESTER

People think that writing a book or even a short story isn't that difficult. Many say that they want to write a book, but that they just haven't started. Most people that say this never will. it's a pipe dream that they spout when someone else says that they're a published author. It's a bit like when I say I have 23 years of martial arts experience. Someone will always say, "I did karate up to X belt." It's usually never up to black belt and when you ask them why they gave up they usually shrug.

The people in this anthology have taken their wish to write far further than most aspiring authors. They have looked for a submissions window that appealed to them. They have read the guidelines and formatting rules carefully and applied them to their work. They have not only done that, but they have sat down at a computer, note pad or some other form of device and they have actually written a story.

Many authors stop at that point. They've written the story, but either don't know how to take things further, or don't want to take things further for fear of rejection. That's perfectly understandable. Many people take rejection as a negative thing, usually along the lines of "I must be a poor writer as I was rejected, therefore I shall never submit again." There are a few who - and pardon my French - take their arse in their hands and try to have the last word with the editor. This is not a good thing for someone who wants to be published as annoying editors with snarky emails is a sure fire way to get yourself onto the "avoid at all costs" list.

But these authors, the ones contained within this anthology went even further than most. They submitted, they then accepted the edits that I gave them, they rewrote their stories until I was happy to accept them, and they did so knowing that every step helped them on their path to getting other stories, maybe even novels accepted. And that, dear reader, is why these authors - some already published best sellers, some complete beginners - deserve the title and accolade of author.

I hope that you enjoy reading their stories as much as I did. They have put a lot of work into them, and any mistakes are unfortunately all down to me.

NAS HEDRON

Nas Hedron is an author, editor, and artist who divides his time between Canada and Brazil.

He is non-fiction editor at *International Speculative Fiction*, a free online quarterly devoted to genre fiction that comes from, or prominently features, countries outside traditional North American and Western European sources.

He is also co-founder and principal editor at *IndieBookLauncher.com*, which provides editing, cover design, and e-book production services to independent authors.

Nas is the author of *Luck and Death at the Edge of the World*, *Los Angeles Honey*, and *The Virgin Birth of Sharks*, among other works. His *Fallen World* series has been called "great science fiction" (Ian Watson, author of *The Universal Machine*) and "cutting edge speculative fiction" (Ernest Hogan, author of *Cortez on Jupiter*). His album *Luck + Death: the Soundtrack for the Movie in Your Head*, has been called "simply outstanding" (Minister Faust, author of *The Coyote Kings of the Space-Age Bachelor Pad*). His fiction and poetry have been published in journals in Europe, North America, and Oceania.

His blog and links to his work can be found at www. NassauHedron.com.

LES POUPE'S GRIS

BY NAS HEDRON

Normandy Countryside, Outside Caen – June 1944

One: Heroic War Tales in Forgettable Films

Hidden in a hedgerow, Fowler shifted his weight. Far in the distance, toward Caen, he could hear the sounds of the war. He glanced at the small stone farmhouse, its windows glowing yellow in the twilight. Nothing yet. He put down his rifle and flexed his arms, his fingers. He picked the rifle up again and looked back at the house, but Scotty wasn't in position yet.

Growing up in Toronto, Brian Wilfred Fowler had learned about war through heroic tales in forgettable films. In the movies there was always a narrative you could follow - so far real warfare was nothing like that. There seemed to be no logical thread to anything that happened. Men rushed forward, and then retreated in confusion. Orders were given, then contradictory orders. In his experience, war was a shuffled deck of unconnected moments soaked in panic.

Just this afternoon, he and his fellow soldiers had scattered, taking cover in farmers' fields when a German tank had rumbled past, and he and Scotty had gotten turned around in some woods, losing track of everyone else. If the landing on the beach had been a masterstroke of meticulous planning and precision execution, it was the exception. The snafu in which he found himself was the norm.

Now he saw Scotty in position on the other side of the farmhouse. They'd both panicked a little when they'd first been separated from the others, but they had forced themselves to calm down. They knew what they were supposed to be doing - securing the area around Caen, house by house - and separated or not, by God they were going to do it.

Many of the buildings in the area had been commandeered by the German occupying forces when France had fallen years before, and were now used to billet soldiers or house administrative posts. Others still had French families living in them. Approaching any given building, you could never be sure which situation you'd find.

Scotty waved twice, meaning he'd approached the house and determined that there were two Germans inside. They approach stealthily, Fowler toward the front door and Scotty the back. When they arrived they abandoned stealth and kicked in the doors, rifles ready.

Fowler charged in first. A civilian woman, who'd been serving soup, froze in place. At a table were two Germans in uniform, bowls in front of them. They started to stand, but when Scotty followed Fowler inside and they found themselves caught between two Allied soldiers, they raised their hands instead.

"Which one of you is in charge?" Fowler demanded.

"They probably don't speak English," Scotty ventured.

The older German, who was about thirty, sighed.

"I speak English just fine. I studied in America before the war."

His speech was natural, but accented.

"What's your name?"

"Konrad Bessler. I'm the *Spiess* here, the Sergeant Major in charge of the ten surrounding farms. This is Fuerst," he said, nodding in the direction of his fellow German. "And that's Madame Fournier."

"Both of you on the floor, face down. Keep your hands away from your weapons."

Before they could comply, the back door opened again. Scotty whirled, expecting an attack. Fuerst drew his pistol and fired at Scotty. He missed, hitting a young woman who stood in the doorway, a look of surprise on her face. She crumpled without saying a word.

Two: Je Vous Donne Les Poupeés Gris!

"**E***stelle!*" screamed Madame Fournier. She ran to the girl, who lay in the open doorway.

"What the hell?" snapped Fowler.

Fuerst looked stricken and started speaking in frantic German.

"He thought it was another Allied soldier," Bessler translated, "that it might be our last chance to escape before you gained the advantage of numbers."

"Weapons on the floor," Fowler ordered. "And be very careful about it."

Bessler surrendered his pistol and Fuerst followed his lead.

"Let me examine her," Bessler said. "In America I was studying medicine until the war started."

Fowler nodded. But Madame Fournier, who'd been kneeling on the floor keening, stood quickly and shoved him away, yelling angrily in French. Fowler had a little French from high school in Canada, but she spoke quickly and he could only catch stray words.

"… killed her… Beasts!... just a child…"

He tried to soothe her.

"Madame…"

She slapped him across the face.

"…all you soldiers… beasts!"

She pointed at each of them in turn, her face contorted with grief and rage.

"Je vous donne les poupeés gris!" She thrust her finger at them as she howled. "Tous les soldats de cette guerre! Et la guerre elle-même! Vous êtes tous maudits. *Tous!*"

Her accusing finger swept the room, taking in all of them. Then she seemed to succumb to grief, turning away to lean on the counter where she'd been cooking minutes before.

"What did she say?" Bessler asked.

But Fournier turned back, a large kitchen knife in her hand.

"Mes méchants!" she screamed at the ceiling, "Voici mon sacrifice! Les poupeés gris, je vous en prie!"

She raised the knife to her own throat and pulled it swiftly to one side, sending a gush of blood down the front of her housedress, then fell in a heap.

"Jesus Christ," Scotty yelled.

Bessler ran to her.

"If I had equipment, blood for a transfusion…" he held up his hands. "I can't do anything. What was she saying?"

"First she was yelling about her daughter. How we all killed her. Then she started yelling about 'the grey dolls.'"

"What does that mean?"

"Damned if I know. She shouted 'my wicked ones, here's my sacrifice—the grey dolls, I pray you,' something like that."

That was when Madame Fournier moved, surprising all of them—they'd assumed she was dead. She struggled to shift her weight.

"Let me make her more comfortable at least," Bessler said.

Fowler agreed and Bessler once again knelt beside Madame Fournier, who reached out a bloody hand. Bessler took it, intending to give her some comfort, but Fournier threw back her head and hissed at him, her mouth wide, the gap in her throat bubbling blood. Her face was splashed with gore and her eyes were open, but unfocused and unseeing. Bessler swore in German and snatched his hand back, standing quickly.

Fournier clambered to her feet as well.

"What the *hell*?" Scotty said.

Fournier hissed again, her head lolling, then lurched forward, trying to bite Bessler. Instinctively Fowler and Scotty raised their weapons and fired. Both bullets hit her, one in the chest and one in the shoulder, and she stumbled back against the counter. After a moment she righted herself, aimed her dead eyes at them, and began shuffling forward once more.

For a moment everyone in the room, apart from Madam Fournier, was too stunned to move. Then both Canadians fired again. Scotty missed, fear causing him to snatch at the trigger, but Fowler's bullet hit her in the forehead. Again she was thrown back and this time much of the right side of her head disappeared, brain and fragments of bone spattering across the counter where she'd been cutting vegetables. As she staggered backward, her buttocks hit the edge of the counter and her upper body rocked a little, but she didn't topple. She hitched up one shoulder, as though trying to correct her posture now that her head was unbalanced, and once again stepped forward.

This time both men fired at her head and didn't stop until nothing remained but a stump of spine. Her body stood for a moment longer, one hand scratching at the air in front of her, then finally crumpled to the floor.

"Gott! *Mein Gott!*" Fuerst whispered hysterically.

"Lord save us!" Scotty crossed himself, then did it again.

Three: From a Time Long Before the Romans Were Here

"**A**h, pauvre Estelle."

They all turned back to the open door, Fowler and Scotty pointing their guns at a beefy man with a thick moustache stood gazing at the dead girl.

"Um, qui êtes-vous?" Fowler managed.

"You Breeteesh?" the man asked, ignoring the guns.

"Canadian," Fowler answered.

The man spoke French, but slowly so Fowler could follow.

"I'm Bertrand Doucette." He gestured at the decapitated Madame Fournier. "Isabelle was my sister. Estelle was my niece."

Fowler was on the alert—after all, they had just shot both women—but Doucette seemed more sad than angry. Fowler lowered his rifle and Scotty followed a moment later. Fowler translated what Doucette had said for Scotty and Bessler.

"Alain, Isabelle's husband, died," Doucette said. "You know, the war. He was her great love. Ever since, I thought maybe she went crazy. Tonight I saw the *poupées gris* and I knew for sure."

"You know about this *poupées gris* thing?"

"What's he saying?" Scotty demanded. Fowler shushed him, but gave another quick précis in English.

"Oh yes, I know this. You know what the word means, *poupée?*"

"*Doll*, right?" Fowler answered.

"Yes. It signifies something that looks like a person but has no life of its own. Like in English, um—popput."

"Puppet."

"Yes. *Poupée* comes from the Latin, if I remember. It's been a long time since I studied the *Grimoire des Oncles*. We got the word comes from the Romans, but the *poupées gris* themselves come from a time long before the Romans were here. Even before the Gauls."

"But what are they?"

Scotty and Bessler had been trying to make out what was going on. Fowler again gave a brief English summary. Fuerst ignored everyone, staring at Estelle and muttering in German.

"To most people in this area the *poupées* are a legend," Doucette said. "Something you laugh about in daylight, but fear in the dark."

"But not for you,' Fowler said.

"To a few families, the Fourniers and Doucettes and Cortots, they're part of our heritage, the old religion. Part of a lore than has been passed down, first orally and then in the *Grimoire des Oncles*. You would say in English the *Spell-Book of the Uncles*, but it doesn't mean *uncles* literally. It means the patriarchs, your father and his brothers and their cousins. These were the men who kept the knowledge and passed it on to the children. Since our first conflicts with the Gauls we've kept the knowledge secret—a family matter only, that was our oath. Now I must talk about it, though."

Fowler took a moment to give another quick update to Scotty and Bessler. He noticed that Fuerst was gazing out the window, whispering to himself.

"The *poupées gris* are the risen dead," Doucette continued. "Isabelle summoned *les méchants*, a kind of wicked spirit. Then she sacrificed herself in order to give her spell power, to actually open the door for *les méchants* so they could enter our world. The incantation she used traps the spirit of a *méchant* within a dead person's body, so that the body remains animated. The flesh loses its color, though, which is why they are called grey. The *méchant* takes over the body and kills everyone it can, biting and tearing with the hands. Only cutting off the head, or destroying it completely can force the *méchant* out."

"So the person who cast the spell doesn't have control over them?"

"No, no. They can only dictate which dead will be affected - people of a certain family - or people who commit a particular sin, things like that. But once the *méchant* enters the dead person you can't control what they do. They kill and then the people they kill become *poupées* as well."

"Wait, I know this," Fowler said with a rush of recognition. "This is like that Bela Lugosi movie, *White Zombie*."

"I don't go to American movies," Doucette said.

"It's about a man in Haiti who makes zombies, living dead, like the *poupées*. It's a horror movie, but it's supposed to be based on a real tradition."

Doucette gave a grim smile.

"And where do you think the Haitian tradition comes from?"

"I assumed it was from Africa."

Doucette shrugged.

"Yes and no. Haiti was a colony of France, but in a colony both the colonizer and the colonized influence each other. In Haiti our languages mixed. French was dominant, but it blended with native languages and with the African languages of the slaves. Our biology mixed because we had children together. And our religions mixed. There are zombie traditions from Africa, but in Haiti they are very fierce because they combine African religion with the traditions of *les Oncles*, they use *les méchants*."

Fowler took a moment to translate once more for the others. He noticed that Fuerst was now silently staring at his reflection in one of the windows. Suddenly, Fuerst screamed something in German. All eyes turned to him and he thrust his head forward, through the pane of the window. He screamed again - Fowler caught the words 'Gott' and 'Estelle' - and slammed his head down, impaling his throat on a shard of glass that clung to the frame.

Bessler got to Fuerst before the others and he tried to hold the wound closed, but the man's throat was a mess. He'd be dead in a moment.

"Get away from him!"

Scotty's voice was full of panic. Fowler, who was kneeling beside Bessler, looked back at him. Scotty was pointing his rifle at them.

"Scotty, what the hell?"

"Get away, I've got him covered."

Only then did Fowler realize that the rifle wasn't pointed at him, or even at Bessler, but at the dying man. He exchanged a look with Bessler and they both backed quickly away from Fuerst and stood.

"Is he going to turn into one of those things?" he asked Doucette, who shrugged.

"I don't know. Can you remember what Isabelle said when she recited the curse?"

"It was something like 'All the soldiers of this war, and the war itself. Now you're all cursed.' I think that's pretty close."

"I don't think he's going to change," Doucette said. "I can't be sure, but it sounds like it was really the war she was cursing. It killed her husband and it killed her daughter. I think the curse will transform anyone who dies in battle. But this man committed suicide - it's not the same."

Fowler translated the gist of the exchange for the others.

"But he killed himself because of something he did as part of the war," Scotty objected frantically, still aiming his weapon at Fuerst.

Fowler relayed this to Doucette.

"No, no, no. That's too indirect. He died from suicide, not fighting."

Fowler explained and Scotty slowly lowered his rifle.

"So that's the rule?" Fowler asked. "Anyone who dies while fighting in the war will become a *poupée*?"

"As well as anyone who is killed by the *poupées*, yes."

Fowler felt his stomach churn.

"But - we're in the middle of an invasion!"

Doucette nodded.

"Now you see why I can't keep our tradition a secret any more," he said. "We are in a war and people are dying by the hundreds just in this immediate area, by the thousands in Caen, by the tens of thousands in all Normandy, by the millions around the world."

Fowler quickly gave Scotty and Bessler a summary in English.

"Are you kidding me?" Scotty sounded on the edge of panic.

"There has to be some way to stop it," Fowler said. "If every war casualty turns into one of *those*," he pointed at the headless body of Isabelle Fournier, "and they transform others, then we have to end it right now or soon there'll be no way to end it at all."

"We have to find her talisman and destroy it," Doucette said. "Now that she's dead, it holds all her power. Each of us in the tradition has one."

"Fine, what is it and where to we find it?"

"Isabelle's familiar was an owl - her talisman is a figurine of an owl with its wings spread. It's in the family home, my grandfather's house, about five kilometers east of here."

Four: An Anemone, or So It Appeared

They left the farmhouse, Fowler and Scotty, Bessler at gunpoint before them, and Doucette scouting their course. They picked their way carefully to the main road. The light from the house only reached a few paces from the door, the moon was hidden behind thick clouds, and a fog had come up. Fowler and Scotty each had a flashlight, but they didn't dare use them for fear of attracting the *poupées*.

The Fournier estate lay due east along the road, but the roads were infested with *poupées*, lurching through the countryside in search of prey. Fowler kept them to the brush at the side of the road to avoid the monsters. Between the dark and the fog visibility was bad, but they concealed themselves nonetheless just to be sure, pausing behind hedges, within clusters of tall grasses, and behind bushes and trees.

They had travelled about three kilometers when they reached an area where the brush at the side of the road became impassable. Fowler halted them and brought everyone together.

"We have to take the road for a while," he said "but we have to be careful. If you think there's something wrong, get off the road and signal everyone else. Whistle—it's not perfect, but it's less conspicuous than shouting."

They set off again, this time walking along the road. They stuck mostly to the edge, trying to remain as close to cover as possible in case they needed to hide quickly. Soon, though, they had to venture into the middle of the road to get around an abandoned hay wagon whose hazy silhouette loomed up out of the fog and shadows.

The huge cart towered above them as they made their way around it. Its base was as high as a man's chest and its cargo was contained within sturdy sideboards that reached just above their heads. These were topped by rails that reached as high again on either side. They stuck close by it, using it for cover despite a foul smell that clung to it - dung maybe, but mixed with something uglier. Fowler saw Doucette swipe a hand at his hair, as though one of the bits of straw jutting out of the wagon had brushed him, but his hand was suddenly jerked between the rails and deep into the wagon.

Doucette shrieked.

There was no point in further stealth. Fowler and Scotty both turned their flashlights on the wagon. It didn't contain only hay. As best he could guess, the Germans had been using it as a makeshift trailer to transport prisoners earlier that evening, maybe fifty of them, then decided it wasn't worth the effort and shot them instead.

Inside the wagon, glimpsed through the rails in the narrow beams of the flashlights, squirming in the foggy night air, was what looked like a monstrous anemone—a solid mass of *poupées* from which a hundred arms sprouted. Perhaps they'd been dormant in the absence of food, but now that prey had wandered near they waved and snatched through the rails and here and there they protruded from gaps in the sideboards.

Doucette was wrenched off his feet and pulled abruptly into the writhing mass, until only his legs and butt protruded, one of the rails snapping to allow his ample belly through. His legs still kicked, but Fowler could imagine what was happening to the rest of him and knew it couldn't go on for long. Scotty tried to help, only to be caught himself. The grasping hands latched onto his arms and cavernous mouths opened as he was lifted off the ground and pinned, cruciform, against the outside of the cart, facing Fowler. Fingers and teeth began to rip the flesh from his arms and back. There was no way to approach him without being caught.

"Shoot goddamn it!" Scotty screamed.

Fowler raised his rifle, aimed at Scotty's head, crossed himself quickly, and fired, killing him before the *poupées* could torture him any further or, worse, transform him into one of them. Then he fired several times at Doucette, though the man's legs had now stopped moving.

The *poupées* lost interest in the dead men. They released their hold on Scotty and his body dropped in a heap. Doucette took longer, sliding slickly out of the anemone and falling to the ground, like a foal being born. Then he hissed hungrily and began to move. Fowler opened fire, not stopping until his head was gone.

Fowler looked at Bessler, who shook his head. Without a word they continued east.

After half an hour a large stone building bulked up out of the night. It was clear they had come to their destination. Their boots grated on the stone steps as they climbed to the front door and entered.

There was no talisman inside. The place where it had stood was clear enough in the beam of Fowler's flashlight. On a set of shelves they could see small hand-lettered paper labels. One read "Hibou, Isabelle"—*Owl, Isabelle*. But the house had been commandeered as a field office and the shelves held nothing but administrative records written in German. Bessler said that it was common for the occupying soldiers to loot artworks and other valuables. They did a circuit of the house, but it was devoid of magical figurines.

Fowler and Bessler emerged to find that dawn had broken and the fog had begun to lift. Dispirited and unsure what to do next, they sat down on the front steps.

Then Fowler heard the faint sound of an engine and looked up. A British Spitfire was levelling out for a strafing run. He looked around for the target and Bessler pointed to a copse of trees on the side of a hillock where two *poupées* in German uniforms stood utterly still, hidden from above by the foliage.

They waited for the plane to blast the *poupées*, but it had lost sight of them and arced back up into the sky. The two men stood, disappointed, until a German tank crested the hill from the other side and drove full bore into the copse, crushing trees, *poupées*, and everything else in its path. Fowler and Bressler cheered and slapped each other on the back. The tank turned and climbed back over the hill, disappearing from sight.

"They're working *together*!" Fowler said.

It appeared that, even without a history lesson from Doucette on the arcane art of the *poupées gris*, military commanders on both sides had quickly determined how the *poupées* worked—and how to kill them—and had united to stop them.

"You know, I'm glad we didn't find that owl," Fowler said.

"Why?"

Bessler was fishing in his pockets for a cigarette.

"Because if we ended the curse, the war would just continue. This way I'm not sure it can. The more people each side kills, the more *poupées* they have to deal with—there'd be no end to it."

"You think the war will end?"

Fowler shrugged.

"We can hope."

———————————

Five: Prosperous, Peaceful, Oblivious
Caen, France (Reich Administrative Zone) – June 2014

Chris Fowler finished his story on that image: his grandfather and Bessler sitting, smoking, and watching the plane and the tank hunt *poupées* together.

"Seriously, there is *no* way," Eric Weiss said. "You are cuckoo."

Normally they'd have been speaking in German, but Eric wanted to go to university in the United States one day, so they were practicing their English.

"Believe whatever you want," Chris said. "My granddad was there. He *saw* it, he was *part* of it. Later he met my granny Élodie, so he stayed here instead of going back to Canada."

"Have you not been listening to Mr. Dreyer in history? There was a truce."

"There wasn't a truce," Chris shot back, "there was a cease-fire—it just ended up lasting a long time. The war isn't even over now, officially. Besides, *why* was there a cease-fire?"

"Old man Hitler saw the writing on the wall," Eric said, "simple as that. He was wily. He'd never have survived the war after D-Day and he knew it."

"No way! Were *you* not listening in history class? Hitler didn't know *how* to say no to a fight. He had a deal with the Soviets for them to stay out of the war and he attacked them anyway. That's not a guy who agrees to a cease-fire just because of the landing at Normandy"

"Wait," Eric said, "you said the thing was an owl?"

"Yeah, with its wings spread." Chris held out his arms.

"Tante Gitte has a thing like that. She said her father bought it during the war."

Chris scoffed, but the two boys went down the street to Gitte's anyway to be sure.

Brigitte Weiss, Eric's aunt, greeted them at the door.

"What do you boys want?" Gitte asked, smiling.

"Tante Gitte, can we look at your old stuff in the attic?"

"If you're careful," she said, holding the door open. "I don't want you boys getting hurt."

"We'll be careful," Eric said cheerfully.

In the hallway upstairs Eric used a cord to pull down a retractable metal staircase that unfolded from the ceiling. The attic was a space filled with boxes and stacks of miscellaneous junk, the detritus that washes up on the shore of any family's life.

The walls were unfinished wood and a pair of bare bulbs hung from the ceiling.

Eric walked to one end of the room and began moving boxes. Chris wandered over and stood behind him.

"There! See?"

A black and grey wingtip protruded from behind a wooden chest.

"Help me get this out of the way," Eric said.

Chris bent down and took one side of the chest while Eric took the other. They moved the chest, revealing a much larger owl statue than Chris had expected. They each took one wing and lifted it gingerly.

Suddenly a red squirrel, which had taken refuge in the attic, darted directly at Eric and ran up his pant leg before panicking and leaping off. Eric panicked too, and instinctively pulled away. The boys lost their grip on the owl, and it dropped, both wings breaking off.

"Oh no, holy crap,' Eric said. "Help me get it back and we'll prop the wings in place. No one will notice."

Eric seemed frantic, but Chris needed a moment.

"Just a sec. I got something in my eye," he said, and sat on the wooden chest facing away from his friend. Through one of the small attic windows he could see the streets of Caen outside, a city that hadn't known war in seventy years. All those years ago his grandfather had failed to end the curse, and that had turned out to be a blessing. As a result this city had grown into what it was now: prosperous, peaceful, oblivious. Chris rested his face in his hands so Eric wouldn't see that he had tears in his eyes.

Six: The Philosophical Problem
Moscow, USSR (Red Army Special Projects, Meeting Room B) – June 2014

There were eighteen civilians and two military secretaries seated around the conference table. Afternoon sun slanted through the window.

"We're going in circles."

"Again."

"Not again - still!"

"Comrades—" Vasylyev said quietly. It was the first thing he'd said since they started. He had no rank or title that they knew of—no-one even believed that Grigory Andreyevich Vasylyev was his real name—but they knew what they needed to know: he was here on the direct orders of the new General Secretary of the Communist Party of the USSR, who had taken a personal interest in the project and wanted his own man on the team.

Minkov, the new General Secretary, had only just taken office. He was one of the post-Glasnost "new Communists," with a bright smile, a Twitter feed, and a Dutch wife, but like any Soviet patriot he still viewed a final victory over Nazi Germany not as a lost cause situated somewhere in the past, but as a dream to be fostered for the future. To make that dream come true, though, they had to get around the *Poupée* Syndrome and the cease-fire it had necessitated.

"Gentlemen," Vasylyev repeated, "and ladies. We need to return to first principles."

"With the greatest of respect Comrade Vasylyev," said Ivanovich, a medical doctor, "we have returned to first principles several times over the years."

"You," Vasylyev said, pointing at a slim man near the other end of the table, "you're Denisoff, the epidemiologist, right?"

"Yes Comrade," Denisoff said. He was a dapper man who was unfazed by anything, even the General Secretary's emissary, and the only person at the table who wasn't visibly nervous.

"You came up with this hypothesis about a microbial toxin—a poison produced by germs or viruses, if I understand correctly. So, what happened to that idea?"

Denisoff shrugged.

"It was a good theory," he said, "it just wasn't correct. We have test subjects—"

"These are Germans?" Vasylyev interrupted, scrolling through some documents on his tablet computer - a brand new military grade *Novy Mozg* he'd just bought - to remind himself of the highly classified test procedure.

"Mostly Germans, plus a small population of Japanese. All descended from prisoners who were in custody at the time hostilities ceased. Originally we used captured soldiers, but of course those are long dead now."

"And you - what? - induce the P-Syndrome intentionally?"

"Wait - what?" said a young man. "You've been keeping prisoners and their descendants alive and *performing lethal experiments on them* and this is the first I've heard about it?"

"Which one are you?" asked Vasylyev, trying to find the right personnel file on his tablet.

"Um - Illiyev, Comrade. From Public Affairs."

"Ah," said Vasylyev, "that explains it. The public don't know, therefore you didn't need to know. But the General Secretary has instructed me to de-compartmentalize information related to this project. He believes it's essential to success."

Illiyev went silent.

"So," Denisoff continued, "we've conducted periodic tests. The mythology around this condition says that the transition takes place whenever there's a violent death resulting directly from the war, so we reproduce those conditions. We have someone from the Red Army shoot one of the prisoners. Technically our countries are still at war, so the conditions are met. When the transition begins we take video recordings. We use contact sensors and we do multiple biopsies before and after the change. But interpreting the results has posed some difficulties."

"Such as?" Vasylyev asked.

"Well, we can't find a biological agent that triggers the change." Denisoff said. "I thought that what we were looking at was an epidemic where the infected person didn't become symptomatic until the pathogen was triggered by some physiological change that would come near the point of death. The person would seem normal, then, just as they approached death - probably *appearing* to die to lay observers – the pathology would kick in, resulting in aggression, reduced sensitivity to pain, and so on. But," he turned his hands upward, empty, "there is no agent. We've tested everything."

"Humph. What else?"

"We had other models, but nothing that worked, even theoretically," Ivanovich said. "Post-hypnotic suggestion could have a similar effect, but how would it have been administered to so many people over such a large area simultaneously? Some kind of environmental toxin, like the hallucinogenic ergot poisonings from tainted crops that produced apparent madness in the medieval period might also work, but as with the microbial toxin, we can't find an agent."

"There's also the - ah - the philosophical problem," said a woman in her forties. "That disrupts *all* the models."

"Ms. Voznesenskaya," Vasylyev said, glancing again at his tablet. "It's a pleasure to see the Tsiolkovsky Physical Sciences Institute represented here. Have you taken to dabbling in philosophy now?"

His tone was jovial, but his eyes weren't and no one laughed.

"No Comrade. That's just the name that's been given to this issue."

"Which issue?"

"Well, since we couldn't find an agent we had to derive information about the *Poupée* Syndrome by other means. We took the mythology as a starting point. The popular notion is that the change is caused by a supernatural curse, and that the curse is activated any time there's a violent death that results from the war itself - from battle, execution, things like that."

"So?"

"The thing is Comrade, over the years the prisoners developed their own allegiances and enmities. So we intentionally managed their living conditions in such a way as to heighten those conflicts. Eventually one prisoner killed another, which was the point of the experiment. His death came about *indirectly* because of the war, but the immediate circumstances that killed him had nothing to do with the hostilities. A curse would know the difference, a biological agent wouldn't."

"And he didn't change?"

"He didn't change, consistent with the mythology. The so-called philosophical issue is: how could a physical process distinguish between the two deaths?"

Vasylyev was losing patience.

"Seventy years ago" he said quietly, "we were poised to defeat Nazism. Because of the *poupées*, we were blocked. Adolf Hitler," here his voice rose "who should have been tried for war crimes and executed like a dog, died at the age of ninety surrounded by his loving grandchildren. The General Secretary can't do anything about Hitler, but he damned well intends to be the leader who finally crushes the Nazis. And *anyone* who gets in his way - including those who fail to provide information we need when it's their job to do so - are going to be in an unhappy situation. Clear?"

There was a chorus of "yes Comrade" and the meeting broke up. Vasylyev noticed his aide, Vysotsky, loitering just outside the door. He crossed to the young man, pulling him aside.

"Comrade," Vysotsky said in a quiet voice, "our problem may be solved."

"What do you mean?"

Vysotsky held up his own tablet, which was open to a video. He hit play. On the screen was one of the test subjects. There were wires attached to electrodes on his chest and to a skullcap on his head. Someone off-screen shot the man in the chest and he slumped against his restraints. Vasylyev had seen videos like it before.

"So?"

"Keep watching."

Vasylyev did, and a strange thing happened: the man stayed dead. No *poupée*. He grinned.

"This was just this morning," Vysotsky said, excited. "I ordered them to repeat the test and they confirmed the results. We don't know what happened, but it seems to be gone."

"Contact the General Secretary's office and tell them I'm on my way."

Vysotsky left and Vasylyev returned to the conference room.

"Ladies and gentlemen, sorry to delay you, but I have some new orders."

There was some confusion and shuffling, but in a few moments everyone had retaken their seats. Vasylyev remained standing.

"I am happy to announce that the *Poupée* Syndrome has ended."

The people at the table looked at one another.

"Then what do you need us to do?" asked Voznesenskaya.

"Exactly what you were doing before: identify the mechanism of the Syndrome. You will have to rely on existing data since there will be no new cases."

"This is prophylactic?" asked Denisoff, "In case there's another outbreak?"

"No Dr. Denisoff. Now that the Syndrome is gone, we will end the cease-fire. We will once again be actively at war with the Reich and in *that* battle there is no weapon too terrible to consider." He leaned on the table, enunciating for emphasis. "I want the *Poupée* Syndrome back, but this time I want it under *our* control, affecting those *we* select."

There was a moment of silence.

"Find the mechanism," he said. "Use science. Use a magic spell for all I care. But find it and figure out how to control it. Starting tomorrow we are going to *bury* the Reich under dead bodies—and whoever controls those bodies will control the battlefield."

STEWART HOTSTON

Stewart crawled out of his grave nearly forty years ago and, thanks to great make up, has been hiding in plain sight ever since. He tends to be pre-occupied with finding enough human flesh to eat and not getting caught while doing so, but in those rare moments when he's not driven to slaughter he loves writing.

LOVE IS STRONGER

BY STEWART HOTSTON

The shells blew out the last of the windows, their booming insistence rushing through the house like an angry child. Louis could feel it on his skin, soft and insubstantial as his mother's fingers. Her body was in the drawing room, crushed under a lintel by the ruined fireplace. He couldn't find the courage to go and sit with her now that the water pooled around her body and her stomach bloated unnaturally. He wondered if a baby might burst forth from her like it had for his aunty Annabelle. He shivered miserably.

His father had been outside foraging when the shelling started. Louis sat in the basement of the house, at the bottom of the stairs, hungrily waiting for the sound of the back door being pushed open that would let him know his father had returned. They had developed a way of opening the door that his father always used when he went out so that Louis would know it was him and not the Germans making a search for survivors.

The late summer had given way early to an autumn that curled its fingers around their village in a firm embrace. Chill air seeped down the steps. Louis passed the time counting the water dripping from the beams running across the ceiling of the cellar. They ran under the kitchen whose shattered windows allowed the rain to seep in, leaving everything cold and wet even when the sun was shining. The puddles that collected on the tiled floor steadily leeched down into the cellar and Louis had learnt to rely on them to be as steady as a clock piece.

There had been allied forces in the town a few days ago and they'd shared food with Louis and his father. A precious tin of salty pink meat, which they had shared like princes at a feast in one reckless meal, together with the powdered milk, and egg that they'd stashed in the basement along with the other food scavenged from the abandoned houses around them. The soldiers had ruffled Louis' hair, telling him he was a brave boy. Louis understood part of their wonder; he remembered how life had been before the bombs and bullets; other children playing in the street and no one locking their doors. He remembered his mother's face in summer and at Christmas when she drank sherry after midnight mass. He locked his heart up in the past because when he tried to pull those memories into the present it felt as if he would fall apart like a broken egg. His father used to tell him jokes, to try and make him smile, but those days were past and the two of them clung to each other now with little more than brief looks.

A squad of soldiers settled themselves into a house on the far side of the village, keeping watch and ensuring that the road was safe for when the rangers arrived. The young men were astonished to find these two hiding in the ruins and remarked to Louis' father what a good boy he had for them to have made it to the liberation. Louis' father held him close that night, "it's nearly over." he said, his voice delicate with hope. The next two days were spent with the rangers; they were busy like his father was when someone needed to be taken to Lyon in their car. Their presence was accepted and as long as they didn't get in the way the soldiers were nice to them. More than once Louis suspected he was just another piece of the village the soldiers knew they had to deal with and then he wondered if the world would ever return to the way it was.

The summer looked like it would depart with a quiet surrender and, with the prospect of the weather inevitably turning colder, the two of them had discussed moving to one of the houses where the windows were more or less intact. Louis did not want to leave his mother behind, even if he was too scared to go into the drawing room and sit with her. He knew his father went there once he thought Louis was asleep. He hoped they talked about nice things. His father would always say, "Love is stronger than death, Louis."

Rain drummed the world above him and the evening faded

into night. Louis stayed at the bottom of the stairs and held his knees up to his chin, hunger gnawing at his stomach. Later, when the gripes were too much to bare he unearthed their stash and allowed himself a carrot and an apple; fruits of both the summer and a fanatically protected vegetable patch behind their house which had escaped the shelling and the notice of the occasional German patrols that passed through the area. He sat and ate his dinner on his blankets, which were laid out carefully, up against a corner of the room. He decided to lie down and keep warm while he waited for his dad.

He woke early the next morning; he couldn't remember falling asleep. Louis looked over at his father's bed and saw it had not been slept in. A cold conker of fear sat heavily in his stomach and he couldn't move. The sound of his own breathing made him feel alone. For a while he played with a tin car, which still had a few scrapes of red paint on its side, pushing it around and around. It made a small scraping noise against the stone floor that steadily grew louder until he threw the car against the wall and strode to the bottom of the stairs.

Louis could hear his father's voice reminding him not to come up to the kitchen until he returned. It was how they said goodbye every time he went scavenging for supplies. His father wasn't there and Louis knew he had to be a big man. He had to be brave and climb the stairs even if he did get in trouble. He prayed he would get into trouble; that his father was testing him and would, after he said sorry, hug him so tightly he wouldn't be able to breathe.

He stepped into the kitchen. A light mist of drizzle blew in through the window over the sink in fitful bursts. Everything was as he remembered it. The sink was shattered and the doors on the cupboards hung open, warped and peeling. Louis walked over to the back door and pulled it open. The garden was filled with the sound of birds. Overhead a flock of geese circled, their honking a warning to all that autumn was coming.

"I'm coming." said Louis to the wind. He searched the garden first, careful to keep an eye open for unexploded shells and to listen for the click of mechanisms that were still trying to complete their only task and explode their payload. Once he had done there he thought about where his father had been looking for food more recently. He remembered a discussion about a family from Gascony who lived on the far side of the village. His father thought they grew potatoes and cabbage. The house was a couple of lanes over from where the allies had settled themselves in. He crept through the streets but saw no one. He found the house and walked through the burnt out cottage into their back garden. A basket of cooking apples was laid on its side, apples burst and scattered across the ground. The vegetable patch was turned over, someone had dug there recently and a small pile of plants lay piled to one side. The rain had flattened the clods into soft sods of mud and weed. Louis walked out to the scene and turned around to look at the cottage The thatched roof had burned off months ago. His father wasn't in the garden, but he had been there when the shelling started.

He traipsed into the house and started to search the ground floor. He had come through the hallway and kitchen so turned off into the first room at the back of the house. It wasn't obvious from outside but a shell had obliterated the floor above and the ceiling had collapsed into the room. His father lay, legs splayed out at odd angles in the farthest corner from the door. Louis knew he was crying but couldn't remember ever having stopped. He crouched down by his father and clasped him around the chest. He pulled one of his, now heavy, arms around him. It lay, leaden, on his back. Louis lay there for a time past counting and the day was drawing in when he found he needed to move. He was at a loss over where to go. He thought about their house but the place was a tomb for him now.

He thought he would go and see the soldiers. They were grownups and they would know what to do.

He clambered up from his father and said "Good bye papa. I love you so much." He touched his father's lips with the tips of his fingers and made a kissing sound.

The soldiers eyed him when he arrived and asked where his father was. "Dead." said Louis.

The men drew him in with a cup of coffee and one of them,

Ned, made him scrambled eggs. They talked quietly in a language Louis didn't know, their gaze turning to him when they thought he wasn't watching.

He swept his plate clean and waited quietly for something to happen. The conversation among the soldiers rose in volume; one of the men was surrounded by the others who were trying to calm him down. Each time the discussion found a lull he would point in Louis' direction and plead, or shout, or shake his head vigorously. Louis wanted to hide but didn't know where to run to, the sun had set and he wasn't sure he knew the way home.

Eventually the men stopped talking, the angriest of them left alone while the others went about their tasks. They checked their emplacements, tidied away supper and settled in with tattered letters, books or their rifles.

One of them brought over a rolled up sleeping bag and dropped it in front of Louis. The soldier squat down and asked, "Do you know how to read?"

Louis nodded and he found a comic pushed gingerly into his hands. "I think you'll enjoy this."

Louis unrolled his bed and climbed in, suddenly tired. Around him the noise of the living going about their business was a sweet lullaby.

The first shot hit cloth with the sound of the fluffing of a pillow. Someone let out a surprised sigh and a body collapsed. The men around him shouted in sudden panic.

Moments later the repetitive staccato of machine gun fire sounded, followed by the sharp cracks of brick and mortar being peppered by bullets.

Louis turned in his sleeping bag but stayed laid flat on the ground. He knew he was safer laying down than trying to run for cover. He unzipped himself in case the time came that he needed to run away.

He watched as two of the soldiers took defensive positions a few feet away, using a low wall as cover from which to try and locate the source of the shots. The other soldiers were scattered around their position and Louis remembered that two of them had been away when he'd arrived.

Ned lay dead on the ground, a crimson stain turning his green fatigues a muddy brown.

The soldiers exchanged fire with their enemy. Louis knew it was the Germans. The Nazis his father called them.

"They hate people." he'd explained one time before the war had found them.

"Which people?" asked Louis.

"Everyone Louis. They hate everyone. Right now they hate people who can't speak German or don't have blue eyes. If they win they'll destroy everything that's beautiful in the world, and then they'll destroy each other."

"So they will lose?"

His father had shaken his head at the question, "No. If they destroy everything they will have won."

The sound of gunfire thinned out as, one by one, the soldiers were wounded or killed. Louis counted the different sounds and realised there were less Germans attacking than there had been. The soldiers might win yet. The two by the wall were firing at a target to their right when a grenade fell just behind them. Louis shouted "Watch out!" and hid his head inside the sleeping bag.

There was a whoomp and the boy was rolled over by the explosion. He looked out of his sleeping bag and got to his knees. The two men were lying still in heaps by the wall. A few bullets were fired into their position but no one was shooting back. Louis knew it was time to go and, getting to his feet, ran around the back of the position and into one of the burned out houses in which the soldiers had been sleeping. Shots ricocheted off the doorframe as he plunged into the house.

There was shouting behind him and more shots peppered the building. He climbed over a broken table and hid there until the shooting stopped. The sound of footsteps on rubble could be heard from the camp and so he looked over the lip of the fractured furniture to see if he could learn what was going on.

He was just in time to see the Nazi soldiers shoot the prone soldiers who were still laid against the wall. A single shot to the face for each of them. Louis screamed in terror. The noise of his fear brought the German's attention around to where he was hiding.

He shouted something sneering in Louis' direction but he knew they couldn't see him. He prayed and called out for his dad. Fear ran through him like water, taking who he was with it and leaving a shiver of incandescent hopelessness.

The footsteps drew closer; they sounded as if they were just outside the house. Louis shifted in his hiding spot and tried not to breathe. Images of his father's body lying dead flashed in front of his face to be followed by the moment the soldier's bodies jerked when they were executed. He pictured his father getting up from where he lay and slowly stumbling towards Louis' hiding spot to help him. These dreams of what could not be were a source of strength and with a click inside his head he knew where he wanted to go.

Louis waited until the Germans started talking to one another and darted towards the back of the house. He ran out of the front door; the wind caught it, slamming is shut behind him and raised voices followed in his wake. The air was cold and damp in his mouth. He kept running until he found the burned out cottage. Pursuing voices were not far behind but he'd made his mind up and did not care.

He ran into the room where his father's dead body lay and stopped. His dad was gone. A whisper that came from everywhere said, "I love you."

Louis turned around but couldn't see anyone. The Nazi's were outside the house. He could hear them talking to each other, making no effort to hide their presence.

He ran out into the back garden and found the scene as he 'd last left it - potato patch partly excavated, apples lying scattered nearby.

"Halt!" came a shout and Louis saw a German levelling a rifle in his direction as he fled back into the house. Bullets hit the wall by the door as he ducked inside. He folded himself into a corner in the kitchen, held his knees close to his chest and waited.

German voices again, front and back this time. The front door opened and someone called out, "Kleinen kinder?"

He knew better than to trust them. He had seen what they did to those children they'd caught in the village. They were murdered just like their parents. He also knew that they'd find him; he'd come here to be found, but his father wasn't here to hold him.

There was the sound of breaking glass from another room just as a shadow fell over him.

"Er ist hier!" shouted the man stood above him; he was grinning.

The door into the kitchen from the hall opened and the German looked up, his pistol slackly pointed toward Louis. Louis closed his eyes and wished he had found his dad.

The soldier gasped and fired his gun twice before there was a sound of thumping and wrestling. Louis kept his eyes screwed up tight waiting to die. A gurgle like a bath emptying sounded in a long drawn out sigh. Louis opened his eyes a fraction and saw his dad standing over one of the Germans. He had his hands around the man's throat. The soldier's eyes bulged in a frozen expression of fear and anger.

Slowly he let go of the man's neck and the Nazi slumped to the ground, getting caught on a cabinet door and hanging awkwardly, his legs splayed out at odd angles.

Louis jumped up and hugged his father around the legs. Hands were placed on his shoulders and gently pulled him away. He looked up at his dad's face and saw the same injuries he had seen earlier except that now his father's ear hung loosely from his skull and there was a ragged wound in his shoulder.

"Andreas?" A voice from the garden called into the house. "Andreas!"

Louis' father ruffled his son's hair slowly and with great tenderness before he limped out into the garden.

The soldier shouted for him to stop and then tried to shoot him. Louis watched from the doorway. His father shuddered as the German fired repeatedly, each bullet hitting him square in the chest; he made no effort to dodge the incoming shots. At the last moment the soldier tried to back away but it was too late. His dead father reached out and grasped the man by his arms and lifted him off the ground. The German shouted then, a raw scream of confusion and terror; he wriggled and squirmed but Louis' father held him firm as he walked towards the apple tree. He stood before an old dead branch that stuck out horizontally at head height and, lining up carefully, shoved the German straight at it. Louis looked away but heard the life go out of the soldier.

Distant shouts could be heard coming from where the allied soldiers had been ambushed and killed. The gunshots would bring the other Germans to find out what was going on. His father walked back to him. Louis noticed that none of his wounds were bleeding.

He pointed at the house and his mouth opened as if he would speak but no sound came out. Louis started crying but did as he was told. He pushed the kitchen door shut and found his previous hiding place.

He wasn't sure how much time passed, each second was an eternity in its own right. The rain continued to fall and he tried to count the drips but gave up in the hundreds. There were more gunshots, each time a short burst that made him wince and cringe, followed by forbidding silence. Each time Louis expected a German to kick open the back door and kill him.

Eventually there was a sound at the back door; it took Louis a few moments to realise it was the handle turning repeatedly, as if waiting for some answering cry from within. Up, down, up and down. Louis rapped on a cabinet door in answer, his heart a bird taking flight. Trained in days of nervous tension and repetition, he knew to remain still until his father was in the kitchen. If it was a German he would remain hidden rather than popping up from behind the counter and giving himself away. A rasping sound came from the door and it opened with a wet sound as it pushed through a puddle.

Louis stared up as his father appeared in front of him. He ran to him and was answered with a bear hug that lifted him from the floor. "Daddy. I love you daddy." was all he could say over and over again.

From the street came the sound of rumbling and heavy engines. The noise was coming from the west. Suddenly he was being lowered and through his protests he could see his father slowly sinking to his knees, a look of peace settling on his tired and ruined face.

"You were right," Louis said through tears of understanding, his heart bursting with joy and sadness. His father inclined his head questioningly, "You said love was stronger than death."

Louis' dad creased his face in a grimace that he realised was a smile and then gently fell onto his face where he lay unmoving.

The End

IAN HALL

I am Scottish, born in Edinburgh, and spent the first 41 years of my life, not far from my fair and bonnie "Athens of the North".

I now live in Topeka, Kansas, with my wife (bless her), no pets (don't like 'em), no children (all moved out), and with many gallons of homemade wine bubbling as I write.

My biggest achievement to date (apart from the successful parenting of my darling daughter) is my published novel; *"Opportunities: Jamie Leith in Darien."*

I'm not confined by genres, having equal success in Historical adventure, Sci Fi, Fantasy, Horror and hard hitting gritty crime.

I watch far too much football (Don't even think of calling it 'soccer'.) and at times chase a dimpled ball along carefully manicured countryside, with a collection of calibrated, graphite-shafted sticks.

I play guitar and sing in a folk/rock band, and would love to have enough money to tour the world's archeological sites until I'm too old to walk.

I love to write, and enjoy literary challenges of all kinds.

Ok, you can see more here...

Vampire stuff; www.vampiresdontcry.com

My blog is; http://www.jamieleith.blogspot.com

My website is; http://www.ianhailauthor.com

Jamie Leith's website is; http://www.jamieleith.com

Thank you for your time.

PULSE

BY IAN HALL

"**A**ll rise." The court officer's voice rang out in the room, echoing from the bare whitewashed walls, clipping every conversation. I stood to attention, my best suit feeling strange on me after so many years in a laboratory coat.

The courtroom was fairly crowded, the case being a direct projection from the Third Reich Core. Press and public had been allowed to attend, hoping for the usual victory of Reich versus Schmutzig.

Purity versus Jewish contamination; bully against bullied.

The judge appeared from behind me, his thin body striding crisply to his desk on the raised platform. A large swastika flag hung on the wall behind him. He stood at attention behind his desk, a man of supreme power, and thus oozing confidence by the bucket-load.

"Judge Major Wilhelm Hildebrandt residing," the Court Officer resumed his monotone diatribe. "Third Tier Military High Court, on the fifteenth of August, two thousand and thirteen."

The judge settled himself in his large red leather chair, and looked round the room as we all slowly sat down again.

His steely eyes repeatedly scanned the room. He never seemed to linger on any one person, but I felt his eyes touch fleetingly with mine, and they smarted like they'd been struck with fire.

"Case sixteen, dash five twenty-one, dash five," The Court Officer announced as he chalked the number on a small blackboard in the corner. He read from a small piece of paper in his left hand. "Third Reich Core versus Klaus Rorschach. The charge; murder in the first degree."

He saluted the judge, his raised arm snapping at forty-five degrees. "*Heil der fünfte* Führer!" Seemingly satisfied with his

39

performance, he theatrically goose-stepped to his seat in the corner.

I felt Hildebrandt's eyes on me before I looked up. "The defendant will rise."

I stood up smartly, wiping a small piece of lint from the front of my suit, and gave my best stiff arm. "*Heil der fünfte Fuhrer*." Not that I'd really liked the first four anyway.

He ignored me, not returning the salute. "For the record, please state your name."

I cleared my throat with a small cough. "Klaus Katrin Rorschach."

"Occupation?"

"I'm a working professor at Third Reich Core Teknical, near Hanover."

"Aryan Class?"

"One thirty-two." I raised my arm, and showed the 132 tattoo on my wrist. Since the Third Reich Asia court decision in 1987, all citizens had to show their Jewish Fraction. Mine denoted me to be less than 1/32 Jewish; the maximum for my generation to work directly for the state.

"Professor, you are charged with murder in the first degree. How do you plead?"

"Innocent," I felt my voice tremble as I spoke. "That is; not guilty."

He nodded, then consulted his notes. "On the second April this year, you fired an experimental weapon at Colonel Maximillian Fedorf, rendering him dead."

"Yes, Herr Major."

"You admit this, yet you plead not guilty?"

"Extenuating circumstances, Herr Major." I glanced at the floor between us. "It was an accident. As you will see in the documents, the Colonel instructed me to fire the weapon at him."

His brows seemed to furrow on his forehead. "Very well, you have my attention." He swirled his hand in front of his face, encouraging me to tell my story. "Don't take all day."

"Herr Major," I nodded my assent. "Are you familiar with my work on the untoten weapon, the KR-1?"

"Yes, I've read the file, so you don't need to go through all the technical stuff. You were researching a weapon to kill the undead, the American zombies."

"Yes, Herr major. Since the successful infestation of 1949 caused by our V4 rockets, we have tried to develop an efficient weapon against the American Continent Untoten. Since we caused the epidemic, we have tried to find a weapon that does not physically harm the untoten, thus causing infestation of the surrounding countryside with their brains. As you know, both we and the Chinese have tried to invade the American continents on many occasions, but secondary contagion has always been the downfall of all attempts."

The judge nodded, but thankfully still seemed to be interested.

"We needed a weapon to break the brainstem, or corrupt the brain without causing external physical leakage; the actual cause of the secondary contagion. My weapon, the KR-1, performed such a function." I waved at the Court Officer. "I would like to show evidence item one; my prototype weapon."

It sat on a small table, the only physical evidence in the case.

The judge looked at me carefully. "Is it safe?"

"Completely. The power source has been removed, rendering it harmless."

The Court Officer handed the pistol to the judge.

The light in the laboratory seemed distinctly more yellow this morning, the sodium lamps burning just a little dimmer than normal.

With a slight shake in my hand, I turned the small screwdriver just a fraction of a revolution, then nodded at the precise adjustment. Tubes extended from the nozzle to a complicated array of sensors and dials. I flipped the suppressor cover closed and hit the kill switch; the trigger.

POP!

The small copper colored pistol gave a slight hiccup, but my eyes were already on the output of the flickering needles on the dials.

"It went over a hundred!" I threw myself onto the back of my sturdy iron chair. Almost as if the sides of my mouth protested the expression, I smiled for the first time in days. "I need coffee!"

In seconds, a trembling cup atop a dirty saucer got pushed onto my workspace. The dark liquid had already spilled from cup to saucer, but I felt reluctant to hit the already cowering pleb. She vanished as soon as she'd arrived, probably grateful somewhere deep down in her psyche.

As my lips pulled on the thin brew, I mused on my creation.

In some fit of vanity, I'd called it the KR-1. Georg J. Luger had achieved fame for his P08 pistol, the very frame my own weapon had been built on. Heinrich Ehrdhardt had achieved fame for his machine guns, eventually selling the Spandau MG 34 all over the world. Why shouldn't I have just a vestige of say in the naming of my creation?

I leant back to the bench and opened the cover again. With the same small-tipped screwdriver, I placed a dab of glue on each of the dials to seal the potentiometers in place.

Then I uncoupled the gun from the test bench and wrapped it in a satin cloth, carefully folding it over the muzzle and handle. I placed it in a cardboard box, with an elastic band holding on the lid, then into the briefcase at my feet.

The judge looked at my weapon. For all practical purposes, it looked like a standard Luger P08, 9mm standard, but of course, but to achieve a separation of classifications, I had changed the color to a nice brushed copper. And, of course, there were 'extras'; a small pipe or two, curling round the thin barrel, two extra knobs near the safety, and of course, the small light bulb looking device screwed into the base of the standard milled wooden handle.

A small triangular shaped suppressor cover sat where the shell cases would normally have been expelled.

"This is a real weapon?" Hildebrandt asked.

"Yes, Herr Major. This is the actual weapon that killed Colonel Maximillian Fedorf."

The judge examined the pistol intently as he waved for me to continue.

"It is a pulse weapon, firing a form of magnetic frequency at the target. The 'pulse' is finely calibrated to find untoten brainwaves, and disrupt the tissue to such an extent that it physically shakes itself apart. It only takes a fraction of a second. The sensor inside was fine-tuned to not affect normal human brain tissue, but that is another story."

He looked over the gun at me. "Tell me of the first trials; where were they held?"

"Can I approach you, Herr Major? I must speak off the record."

He initially seemed impatient to get on, but he did motion me with his finger.

I crossed the room and bent far over his high bench, whispering so only he could hear. "Herr Major, to do so, I have to keep the location of the first trial from the record."

"And why is this?" His brows furrowed.

"Herr Major, for the very first trial firing, the untoten were brought to a Danish Island."

"In Europe?" He hissed at me. "This breaks many laws and treaties."

I swallowed, determined that I be heard despite my 132 status. "Nevertheless, Herr Major, the location has no relevance to the case. Please do not ask me on record to say where it is. I wish to neither divulge the secret nor perjure myself."

He nodded, and flicked his head, a dismissal to my own table.

———————

Once outside, I pulled my cuffs down to my wrists and walked determinedly to the car. The '132' tattoos once again hidden. The black Mercedes looked stark in the harsh white light of morning.

The uniformed driver's epaulettes showed him to be dirty Wehrmacht, content unknown.

Maybe even a schmutzig like me.

"Aerodrome." I said, then leant back on the seat, wallowing

in the comfortable grey leather, yet reminded of the thin veil separating me from the schmutzig doing the driving.

The tattooed numbers on both wrists gave away my Jewish ancestry, yet if I hadn't been involved in research, weapon research in particular, our tables could have been firmly turned. He would wear the sneer, and I would have my head lowered in the now traditional position of subservience.

Captain Mercier met me at the steps to the plane, and pointed to my briefcase. "It's finished then?" his boyish charm dissipated any doubts of his loyalty to the cause.

I wondered at the extent of his intelligence as I shook his hand. "You are well informed, Captain."

"The pleb."

I smiled grimly, I should have known better. The Reich high command would scarcely allow me to work totally unsupervised. "Of course. It is sufficiently ready to test. Do we have something to shoot at?"

"We have the untoten targets in place, delivered fresh from America this morning."

His simple statement belied the logistical nightmare involved. Due to many trade and medical treaties with the rest of the countries in Europe, untoten were totally forbidden.

"How many?"

"We were allocated ten." He stepped up the ramp, and into the shiny silver plane. "Will that be sufficient?"

"Yes, completely." I followed him inside the small plane.

Ten 'untoten'; individual zombies ripped from the fabric of a whole continent of undead, probably individually boxed to prevent harming themselves. Then flown to meet me; the grandson of a Jewish 'hure', killed in Belsen in 1952. I gave myself a mental shake, as I walked behind this Aryan masterpiece. I was less than one thirty-second Jewish, my tattoos said as much, and it held enough stigma to colour my thoughts every day.

I had been saved by the Feinstein act of 1998, saved by the coalition of Reich and fad. It seemed that after disposing of all one sixteenth schmutzig, the movement had suddenly become tuned to a higher power; that of world opinion.

And at the last minute, I had escaped the cut.

Inside, once we'd gotten airborne, a very blonde stewardess brought us fresh sandwiches, Danish cheese, and a bottle of the finest French champagne. Considering the short transit time, it felt like celebration indeed. Apart from Mercier and myself, the small elegant plane carried no other passengers.

"Can I see it?" he asked, leaning back in his seat, blowing rings of cigarette smoke high into the pressurized cabin.

I shook my head. "It's not safe in here." I imagined the thin gossamer webbing inside the airplane's walls. "Not enough margin for error. Sorry."

"Oh, I suppose I'll see it soon enough." His grin looked authentic.

Just then, the engines relaxed considerably, announcing the halfway point of our journey. I looked at my watch, making sure the cuff did not ride too high. Eleven minutes to travel two hundred miles.

True German engineering.

I made a conscious effort to look the judge directly in the eye. "Well, Herr Major, the small adjustments always took the longest time. But the Reich High Command was restless for some form of breakthrough. The first superpower with a clean untoten weapon would be able to encapsulate the Americas. Imagine the wealth of two continents coming exclusively to the Reich. The sudden riches would dominate China for decades."

He nodded, and waved at me to continue, seemingly frustrated at the speed of my testimony.

"The lab tests could go no further; we needed a proper field test. It didn't matter how deadly a weapon happened to be, if it didn't work just right, or the magnetic pulse didn't go exactly where the sights said it would, it could prove useless in the field. So we tested it…"

"Let it be known for the record," the judge interrupted, his voice suddenly over-amplified, filled with squealing feedback and bouncing off the walls. "That the location of the test is classified."

"I have a film of the trial, Herr Major."

On a nod from the judge, the courtroom lights dimmed, and a screen appeared in the wall to my right.

The film, shot by Captain Mercier, showed me standing on a gantry over a small field. I motioned to the camera to turn to the field, and with a swift jerk, it showed the zombies in the field. One by one they became aware of our presence, and began their drugged shamble toward us.

The camera now looked down my arm, the KR-1 now aimed at my first target.

"I will now fire the weapon." My voice sounded off screen.

"Pop." Hardly a noise at all, more like a quiet beer being opened.

When the nearest untoten began to fall, the camera focused closer on them. No noise, no recoil, no tissue breakage; one by one the zombies just dropped to their knees and fell over.

Suddenly the screen flickered and went white.

A cold wind cut through my coveralls the instant I stepped onto the stairway. Even in June, the north Atlantic threw a cold swell eastward. I paused at the top of the steps, shivered, then quickly got down to ground level.

The island even looked small from the ground. No features, no hills, just flat grass, and maybe the suggestion of fences.

A car waited nearby. Nothing expensive this time, I knew for a fact that only four cars existed on the island. It took us to a small fenced compound on the southern edge.

I felt pangs of nervousness fire through me like electrical charges.

Captain Mercier and myself. The only two witnesses to history being made.

I silently resented the fact that we were not mobbed by press and government officials. The Reich needed a private testing, in case it all went horribly wrong. Damn them.

Tall concrete fence posts held the thick chicken wire in place. The car stopped near a gantry.

Inside the fence, the ten subjects stood, disinterested, unmoving.

"What's wrong with them?" I asked as I got out of the car.

"They were probably drugged." Mercier winced at the cold chill. "To keep them docile in transit. Is there a problem with that?"

I also winced, fearing my calculations might be affected by the added drugs. I hoped not. The pistol had been 'tuned' to brain matter, untoten brain matter to be more precise.

I rested my briefcase on the hood of the car and pulled out the cardboard box. I flipped the elastic band onto my wrist, and lifted the lid. I had no idea why I treated it with such care, as I knew its rugged design.

Slowly I unwrapped the gun. The copper finish gleamed in the sunlight, sending shimmering pinpoints of light into my eyes.

Standing on the gantry, the feeling of absolute power that I felt in that moment would never leave me. I pointed the gun, and the subjects fell. After the third victim fell to the ground, I aimed increasingly to one side, first their ear, then past their heads altogether.

They still fell.

Finally on the last two, when I pointed the weapon almost two feet to one side, they still came at me. I tried firing on both sides; nothing.

Finally, as they reached the fence, I pointed the gun downwards at their raised grimaces and fired. Both toppled like I'd hit them on the forehead with a large hammer.

Mercier jumped up and down like a child, his cap becoming loose on his head. He'd lost all semblance of propriety, no longer the Aryan officer, excited in the weapons efficiency.

"Good God," The judge exclaimed quietly. "They are all dead?"

"Completely, Herr Major," The lights rose again. "Extensive tests were done on the cadavers, none showed outward harm, no secondary contagion. All remained quite dead."

He leant back in his chair, with his fingers interlaced. "How are you placed in the Party, Professor Rorschach?"

I noted that he'd given me my professional title. "I am in eminent standing, Herr Major. I earn a very decent wage, and my research facilities are second to none."

"And there is no-one else involved in this research?"

"No, Herr Major."

He looked at me carefully, making notes. "Tell the court what happened next."

"Well, we built ten units, all to my original specifications, all calibrated by me, all tested in my laboratory, all showing the same results. Then we flew to a coastal town just west of Halifax, Nova Scotia."

"Why there?"

"Well, we needed a zombie population untouched by previous invasions."

"I see."

They gave me skilled workers and for once I did no labour on the weapons. But I supervised every solder joint, every small component. I probably worried more over these new weapons than my first, knowing the importance of their function. These would not be used by myself in a field with captive untoten, tenderly kept wrapped in a soft square of linen. These weapons would be fired by soldiers, uncaring of the fragility of the inner workings.

These weapons had to be better than my first prototype.

I got visits from Generals, who asked me to explain the pulse process repeatedly. They asked for my opinions of a rifle version, a machine gun, an artillery application.

In the evenings, I was wined, dined and whored, in a style far above both my station and comfort zone. Although I liked the new peripheral perks, there seemed always to be the feeling of a false summer, a reminder of how gossamer thin my new improved position actually was.

"Tell the court of Nova Scotia."

"In an advisory capacity, unarmed, I walked into town with the ten soldiers who each carried a KR-1. We were accompanied by fifty of the best commandoes for support, but they were never needed. Saint John is a small town. Using just my ten weapons, we killed over a thousand untoten before the power sources started to show signs of overheating. None of the men were harmed, and we left the area within two hours. It was both a total military and strategic success."

"And the weapons?"

"The power units showed signs of overuse. If we continue my research, we will improve them."

"The men in the unit," the judge began, "Did they show any signs of stress or strain in the action?"

"No, Herr Major." I looked down at my notes. "All were given a clean bill of health."

The flight across the Atlantic took three hours; ninety minutes accelerating, ninety minutes cruising to a decelerated speed suitable for landing on an aircraft carrier. The ship cruised in the Bay of Fundy, just off the Canadian coast. Sailors on the deck of the carrier bustled to get us in out of the thick torrential rain. The next day, the weather had lessened, and sunshine and cloud dotted the sky. We set off in two brand new E-boats, the film crew, the obligatory officers, and the ten soldiers, all armed with new pre-production models of my weapon.

The wharfs of the town looked clear of untoten, but the supporting commandoes acted their parts in the documentary, sweeping along the jetty, meticulously rounding vehicles and debris, wary of zombies.

"Klaar!"

The ten men with the new guns, followed by myself, were allowed to move to the front. The officer in charge called for the helicopter, and within seconds it flew overhead, stopping about a quarter of a mile in front of our position. A tape machine playing loud music was lowered, and the chopper left the area. The silence that followed its departure seemed complete. Then, from shop doorways and side streets, they began to arrive. Shuffling, shambling, first towards the noise of the tape machine, then once they'd spotted us, they increased their speed, and approached us.

We toppled them over at a hundred meters, we toppled most at one fifty, and even the occasional shot at two hundred yards brought them down.

Of every zombie felled, none re-asserted itself into the populace; all remained totally dead.

---

66 Tell me of the morning of the second of April this year."

"Yes, Herr Major. Our second trip to Canada proved slightly less successful than the first, and it left us with a new calibration problem.'

He raised his hand. "Is this relevant?"

"Yes, Herr Major. The original calibration no longer seemed valid. I had to re-tune every gun myself, in the field. But soon, we had the problem sorted and the second trial was a similar success. We filmed the whole scene, but it had since been classified."

He looked at his notes, looking slightly perplexed. "But this trip was not April the second?"

"No, Herr Major, this was a week before."

He sighed, never a good sign. "So *please* tell the court, and myself, what happened to Colonel Fedorf."

I could feel my throat beginning to constrict with nerves. "On April the second, we landed at a hamlet just north of Jacksonville for our third field trial. But the calibration problem returned, and again the guns did not initially work well. Three of the team were compromised by the untoten in hand to hand fighting. They were instantly shot. The commandoes helped clear the area, and I got to work, again adjusting to the new frequency for the sample brainstems, of which

I had a few lying around. Satisfied that the pistols again were proficient, we moved into the town, and cleared the area with some proficiency."

I could see the judge becoming more impatient. His voice had slipped to an annoyed monotone. "What happened to Colonel Fedorf?"

"Colonel Maximillian Fedorf was in charge, and after we'd cleared the area of all untoten, he ordered the film crews to monitor one last demonstration of the weapon's capabilities. I pleaded with him to stop, but he'd not hear of it, and I have three senior Reich's officers who will testify to my pleading."

He waved his hand in exasperation. "Irrelevant. Do we have film of this?"

"Yes, Herr Major, but again it is classified."

Bang! Hammer on gavel. "Declassify!"

Bang! "I now declare the film relevant. Play, please."

The cajor stood against the wall of a bar, almost windswept to rubble in the sixty years of dilapidation.

"Come on, shoot!" he cried.

Handcuffed on each side of him, their handcuffs nailed to the wall, two savage untoten struggled to get their hands to the clean meat between them. They snarled and growled, but it seems the colonel was unresponsive to both their passions and proximity.

"Shoot!"

I shook my head again and again, but my arguments had been dismissed so many times, I had no alternative to carry out his order. "Colonel Fedorf wishes to demonstrate the ineffectuality of the guns against human targets."

Pop. One untoten fell, held now only by the nails in the cuffs.

Pop. The second fell, his hips swaying into the colonel's uniform, buffeting him.

Pop. The colonel looked a mite puzzled, then fell forward like he'd been poleaxed.

We all rushed to help, but the colonel was stone cold dead before he hit the cracked grassy cement.

I didn't stand still for a second. The gun was taken from my hands and I got handcuffed, incidentally the same ones just used on one of the zombies.

"You fired the gun?" the judge asked.

"Yes, Herr Major."

"So what went wrong?"

"Herr Major, I cannot answer that question with fact, only conjecture."

"Very well," He leant forward in his chair, baiting me. "So how do you think it happened?"

"I came to my own conclusions, being released from custody to follow up my experiments. In the three weeks from the first trial, to the unfortunate accident involving Colonel Fedorf, it seems that the cranial physiology of the untoten somehow changed to match that of humans."

He gave me a very puzzled look. "Explain."

"I'm not certain that I can, Herr Major." I shook my head in unconscious emphasis. "You see, there's only two ways that a race can alter their internal make-up to the degree that the zombies did. One is by long-term micro evolution."

"And they cannot evolve in three weeks." He said, his voice smug and self-assured.

I nodded. "The second is by an external force."

Again, the puzzled expression. "External?"

"Well, if we neglect the evolution theory as being far too controversial, we must assume that the untoten population have been changed by an unknown force acting on their behalf."

I stopped, knowing that my next supposition would be stretching my own, untested theory.

"Outside force?"

Somehow the words would not come.

"You mentioned an outside force, Professor Rorschach."

"Well," I could tell my demeanour had changed. My shoulders had slumped slightly. "There is the possibility that they have been changed as a species by the short applications of the gun's waves."

His eyes seemed to grow as big as saucers. "So you could be responsible for the altering of the whole zombie population?"

I nodded. "Perhaps even for the good." I countered quickly.

"There's six hundred million of them, perhaps we can cure them, take back what we started."

Looking at me intently, the judge did a little circle motion with his hand, his finger pointing down.

"Court is now dismissed." The court officer shot to his feet.

Hands grabbed me, and with no finesse whatsoever, guided me out the door.

Camera flashes surrounded me, with shouts of 'treason' and 'traitor'.

The men handling me through the doorway gave no thought of banging me against both sides before dragging me to the dark corridor beyond.

"I'm the saviour." I shouted, then realized it may not have been the best thing to say.

Fists pummelled into me, as the world around got darker and darker.

"I am the inventor of the KR-1" I managed to squeak as my jaw got broken, and my lips swelled.

"KR-1" I gurgled, blood filling my oesophagus.

I bet Georg J. Luger never got beaten to death.

GAV THORPE

Joining Games Workshop at the age of nineteen, Gav Thorpe was a staff writer and games developer on the Warhammer and Warhammer 40,000 universe for fourteen years, and has also written novels for the same for the past fifteen years and more. His most popular works include *The Sundering* trilogy, *The Path of the* Eldar, works from the Horus Heresy series including *Deliverance Lost*, the audio dramas *Raven's* Flight and *Honour to the* Dead, and the New York times best-selling novella *The Lion*. He is also published by Angry Robot books where you can find his epic swords-and-sandals fantasy saga gathered in the omnibus collection entitled *Empire of the Blood*. Gav has also worked on, and is currently working on, numerous tabletop and video games, including as a designer, writer and world creation consultant. He lives near Nottingham with his partner Kez and baby boy Sammy.

RISE OF THE SECRET KING

BY GAV THORPE

22:50, 30th April, 1948

The inside of the C-53 transport stank of sweat and oil. The airframe creaked and rattled around the twenty-eight seated men and there was no chatter to break the drone of the engines. Sergeant Leszek Urbanski gripped his Thompson tightly in his lap and watched the other men around him.

Most were strangers, brought in on this mysterious secondment from other paratrooper formations, but he knew Dan 'Lucky' Johnson and Lieutenant Steven Mayhew from his days in the 513th Parachute Infantry Regiment, 17th Airborne. The Lieutenant caught his eye with a grim look, silently sharing the memory of the last time they had sat next to each other preparing for a drop.

Everybody seemed on edge. The briefing had been, well, shockingly brief. None of them really knew what they were doing, preparing to drop somewhere in Germany years after the war had ended. Something to do with the Russians, probably, but the Colonel who had held the briefing had only told them that they had been gathered for a raid against a clandestine enemy position. It would be a night drop – which brought its own perils but Urbanski preferred those to what had happened last time – and from the dropzone they would assault an enemy-held position.

Details were scarce. Number of enemy – unknown. Preparedness of enemy – unknown. Fortifications and emplacements – unknown. Air defences – unknown.

"Relax, Banksy," Mayhew said, leaning over to be heard above the engines. "This isn't Varsity."

Mayhew's words did not reassure Urbanski. His gaze moved to the scrawny man sat at the back of the aircraft; the 'special advisor' from Washington. No department had been given and he certainly didn't look like a soldier.

The diminutive advisor, Weatherall, seemed the calmest of them all. He was swamped in his borrowed fatigues, his helmet perched precariously on his head, but he looked relaxed as he flipped through the pages of a large notebook on his lap.

Weatherall carried it with him everywhere, like it was his weapon or something, but was careful to avoid anyone else seeing what was written within.

Urbanski couldn't quite make out in the dim light what was on the pages. Lines of neat script; geometric patterns and strange shapes in black and red; notes in the margins. Extra sheets were stuffed between the pages, stained and tattered.

"I hope that's details of the enemy dispositions, Weatherall," Mayhew spoke up. 'I'd like to think someone knows what we're doing here."

The small man looked up in surprise, broken from deep thoughts. He smiled and closed the notebook.

"A battle plan of sorts, Lieutenant Mayhew." Weatherall's voice was deep, at odds with his small frame, and carried easily above the noise. As he spoke he patted the book affectionately. "If we are swift and decisive, such matters will resolve themselves."

"You know a lot more than you're telling," said Urbanski. "We're right here, about to drop into whatever's down there. Can't you spare us even a hint?"

Weatherall sighed and straightened in his harness. He carefully placed the book in a thick leather case and fastened the clasps before looking directly at the sergeant.

"Nazis, Sergeant Urbanski."

This drew surprised muttering and a few incredulous laughs from the paratroopers, but Urbanski simply nodded.

"War criminals, I guess," said the sergeant.

"The worst kind, Sergeant Urbanski. The very worst."

A shout through the cockpit door warned that they were nearing the drop zone. The men burst into activity, performing final checks of their parachutes and weapons, rigging up their lines overhead.

Urbanski tightened the strap on his helmet as Mayhew opened the door. Cold wind brought raw air and the roar of the engines into the cabin.

The night was clear but for a few scattered clouds. The moon was barely a sliver in the sky and a glance down revealed nothing of the terrain below. Urbanski saw occasional pinpricks of light; windows of isolated houses and farms it seemed. Not far ahead was the glow from a larger group of buildings.

"Ready up!" shouted Mayhew.

Urbanski stepped forwards, the first to make the jump.

10:03, 24th March, 1945

The sky was filled with explosions. Anti-aircraft fire was tearing into the transports; dozens of planes were burning, trailing smoke and fire, the ruins of gliders dropping down into the fields below.

Urbanski didn't allow himself time to think. He threw himself out, bent slightly forward, feet and knees tight together and chin tucked in to prevent him from tumbling in ungainly fashion. Smoke burnt his eyes but he kept them forced open as he counted.

"One thousand... Two thousand... Three thousand... Four Thousand..."

The jerk of the opening 'chute came as a moment of relief. He looked up, assuring himself the canopy was filled properly. He snatched at riser lines above him, pulling them down sharply. There was clear air around him and he took a deep breath, chilling his mouth and throat.

Slipping to his right, against the wind pushing him away from the landing site, Urbanski had time to see what was happening below. There were gliders on the ground and billowing canopies. The paratroopers he had expected, the gliders he had not.

Someone had screwed up. This was not his landing zone.

There was nothing else to do but do his best to control the descent, turning into the wind as a muddy field rushed up to meet the sergeant. He pulled down his right hand hard and locked his arm, his breath forced back into his mouth as he turned.

He rolled as he hit the ground hard. Scrubby grass and stones scratched at his face and hands as he landed awkwardly, snatching at the canopy release.

He lay on his back for a moment, trying to regain his composure. Above, hundreds more canopies were opening against a backdrop of burning planes and ack-ack fire. In the light of day the German gunners had no problem finding targets.

Sounds of closer gunfire brought his attention back to his own situation. There was no time to relax.

Pushing himself to his feet, Urbanski gathered in his canopy as best he could to stop it entangling the others as they landed around him. He looked around for Lieutenant Mayhew and saw him sitting nursing his ankle about thirty feet away.

Running over to the officer, Urbanski helped him to his feet. The Lieutenant was tight-lipped, eyes narrowed with concern as he surveyed their surroundings.

"We've landed with the Brits, for God's sake," muttered Mayhew. He looked at Urbanski and pulled out his service pistol. "Let's find someone who knows what the hell's going on."

23:13, 30th April, 1948

"This way, quickly," said Weatherall, pointing towards the silhouette of a large castle that dominated the wooded hill ahead. He had his leather case clasped to his chest, cradling it as if the battered bag was a child.

They had landed in a meadow about half a mile from the castle. Urbanski wasn't sure if Weatherall was in charge or not and looked to Mayhew for guidance. The lieutenant shrugged and gestured towards the government specialist, who was already advancing through the long grass at a brisk pace.

"If in doubt, follow the man who acts like he knows what's happening," said the Lieutenant. "Parker, Dixon, flank left. Ferguson, take your men right."

Urbanski and the rest fell in with Mayhew as the nominated men spread out across the field. The sergeant released the safety on his Thompson and swallowed hard. The darkness had a strange edge to it, the trees and castle faintly glimmering in the scant moonlight.

"Seems unnecessary," said Urbanski. "A combat drop, I mean. If there's Nazis here, why not just send some troops in to round them up in trucks?"

"Don't ask me," growled Mayhew, "I just work here."

"Government advisors and secret night drops, it's not normal."

"Stay focussed, Banksy. If there are Nazis here, they won't be pleased with us dropping in to say hello. Maybe the brass wanted to avoid warning them."

They continued in silence, following Weatherall who set a brisk pace. Passing through a line of trees, the man from Washington stopped in the shadows. Mayhew quietly called out the order to halt at the tree line.

The castle was an imposing edifice; a triangle pointing north like a spear tip with a huge round tower forming its apex. Starlight cast a glimmering haze from three main storeys of windows, but from the north tower a sickly light glowed from within.

"South," said Weatherall, pointing to his right. "We have to cross the moat bridge to enter."

"Wait a moment," warned Mayhew, grabbing Weatherall's arm as he made to set off. "Look."

There were figures patrolling back forth across the stone bridge that joined the castle to the south.

"I'll defer to your expertise for the moment," Weatherall conceded.

Quickly and quietly, the lieutenant detailed his men for an assault on the moat bridge. The others slipped out into the trees that grew almost up to the walls of the castle, ready to provide covering fire. Mayhew and Urbanski led a dozen of the paratroopers, Weatherall in tow, directly towards the bridge.

They came to a wall-lined road. About a hundred yards ahead, at the near end of the moat bridge, was a wide stone area on which were parked several nondescript trucks and a battered-looking Daimler. Beyond, an unkempt garden fronted the castle, dropping deep into the dry moat, broken by hedges and trees.

Urbanski counted eight men by the vehicles and seven more on the walled bridge itself. The far end of the crossing ended in an ornate archway, the wooden door within open to allow a pool of light to spread across the stones. Occasional shadows betrayed the presence of more men inside.

"S.S. bastards," rasped Urbanski, recognising the uniforms of the soldiers on guard. "Strutting about like they own the place."

"They used to," whispered Weatherall from behind the sergeant. "This is Wewelsburg, Sergeant Urbanski, once chosen by Himmler himself as the centre of the S.S.."

"You'd think they'd pick somewhere less obvious," said Urbanski. "Did they think nobody would notice them coming back?"

"They have very compelling reasons for coming here, Sergeant Urbanski."

"Surprise and speed," said Mayhew as they paused just within the shelter of the woods.

Following Mayhew, they slipped over a stonewall onto the road. Keeping low, they advanced to within a dozen yards of the parking area. Glancing to his right, Urbanski saw another stick dashing across the road to the south, heading towards the grounds on the other side of the vehicles.

He could hear the muttered exchanges between the patrolling soldiers and tobacco smoke drifted on the wind. Just on the edge of hearing he thought he could hear other voices, dimmed by distance but resonating within the castle itself.

"We'll give Dixon another couple of minutes and then we go," said Mayhew. The lieutenant laid a hand on Weatherall's shoulder. "You stay here, keep your head down, until we've taken the gate. Okay?"

"Just as you say, Lieutenant Mayhew. I will stay right here."

Urbanski's mouth was dry but his grip on his Thompson was slick with sweat. He wiped his hands on his trousers and licked his lips.

He hated this moment. The brief lull before action that stretched out into a lifetime.

Adrenaline was already making his heart pound and he concentrated to control his breathing, eyes fixed on the figures strolling to and fro within a stone's throw. If one of them broke away, decided to come along the road or extended his patrol further south, they would be seen.

———————

13:01, 24ᵗʰ March, 1945

The waiting was over.

"Get into them!" roared Mayhew, waving the squad out of the alley and towards the steps of the German-held townhouse. The street was choked with rubble and nearly all of the buildings to each side had been flattened by successive air raids and artillery strikes.

Machine gun fire rattled from the far end of the street as Urbanski stumbled over the scattered masonry and surged up the steps to the house's front door. Fire sparked from the windows above as he kicked open the front door and didn't stop, barrelling into a German lurking on the far side.

The sergeant acted out of instinct, driving the German soldier sideways into the wall as more of his men pounded past into the house's depths. The soldier spat something in his guttural tongue as he tried to bring up his rifle.

Urbanski thrust the muzzle of his Thompson into the man's gut and fired, shredding his innards, spattering blood across the patterned yellow wallpaper of the hallway. Stepping back he allowed the body to drop. A moment later he followed Lucky up the stairs.

A grenade clunked onto the landing in front of them, right at the top of the stairs. Lucky turned and dived back, dragging Urbanski with him. They tumbled down the steps in a painful embrace as the grenade detonated.

Shrapnel ripped into the ceiling and walls, the noise of the explosion making Urbanski's ears ring. Plaster dust and tatters of gaudy paper showered the pair and smoke billowed down the stairwell.

A helmeted head appeared at the top of the stairs as Urbanski pushed himself away from his companion. Lucky's rifle barked and the German's face disappeared in a welter of blood.

"C'mon, sarge, shake a leg," laughed Lucky, plunging back up the steps two at a time.

Urbanski followed, reaching the landing as Lucky smashed his way into the first bedroom, firing his Garand. The sergeant emptied the rest of the Thompson's magazine into the door at the far end of the corridor and dodged back onto the stairs to reload.

Mayhew appeared in the hallway at the bottom.

"Henrikson, get upstairs!"

Two seconds later another paratrooper was crashing up the stairs to help, following right behind Urbanski as the sergeant launched himself once more onto the landing, finger ready on the trigger.

The door he had riddled with bullets was half-open, something slumped against it from inside the room. There was one more door to clear, on the left facing towards the street, and Lucky was already on the far side, a grenade held at the ready.

"On three?" asked Henrikson.

Urbanski ignored him. The sergeant booted open the door and stepped back in one motion. Lucky tossed the grenade through the opening and they retreated with weapons levelled.

A figure came stumbling from the doorway before the grenade exploded, his camouflage remarkable amongst the grey-fatigued Wehrmacht, his collar badges betraying membership of the S.S.. Recognising an officer, Urbanski managed to knock Henrikson's rifle aside just as the paratrooper fired, sending the shot into the wall.

Lucky was more experienced and smashed his rifle butt into the side of the officer's head as the grenade detonated.

A scream of pain sounded from the bedroom.

"Sit on him," snapped Urbanski, pointing at the Nazi officer while he headed into the room.

The German still in the room had tried to hide inside a

wardrobe but had been too slow. Wooden splinters jutted from his face and throat, his right eye a bloody mess. Urbanski fired into the wailing man's chest, putting him out of his misery.

Shouts from below confirmed that the downstairs rooms had been cleared. Urbanski glanced out of the door and saw the S.S. officer face down on the floor, Lucky's knee in his back. Satisfied that all was under control in the immediate vicinity the sergeant crossed to the window to look outside.

The machine gun had been silenced; other squads were moving through the few houses still standing, sweeping across the piles of broken brick and stone that remained of the rest.

"Bring him," Urbanski said as he exited the room, nodding towards the officer. "Let the Lieutenant decide what to do with him."

Downstairs, Mayhew was standing at a doorway leading into a basement and was directing men to take positions at the windows.

"What you got there, Banksy?"

"Prisoner, Lieutenant."

Lucky shoved the groggy German towards Mayhew, who stepped aside and waved them to the basement steps.

"We'll keep him down there until we can move him back to headquarters. He seems placid enough. We'll hold out here while the Brits push on into the hills, and try to get to the Colonel at nightfall. Wesel is a dead town now, nothing here to bother us."

Urbanski wasn't sure, but he thought he saw the S.S. officer smirk as he was bundled down the steps.

―――――――――

23:31, 30ᵗʰ April, 1948

The attack started with a grenade from Lucky, as the paratroopers reared up out of their hiding places and stormed towards the bridge.

The grenade exploded amongst the trucks, killing two of the guards and sending the rest of the S.S. troopers scurrying for cover.

"You must secure the gate and get inside!" Weatherall shouted from behind as Urbanski and the others pounded along the road.

"Military genius," Urbanski muttered as he dashed along the road.

Dixon and his squad poured fire from the other side of the parking area, filling the night air with the crack of rifles and whine of bullets. Lucky, Dominici and Urbanski stopped at the end of the wall and opened up on the guards who had taken cover behind the parapet running along the moat bridge.

More soldiers were running from the open gateway and were caught in a hail of fire directed by Mayhew, who was now a dozen yards ahead.

"Follow up! Pour it on!" barked Urbanski, surging forwards once more, reloading his Thompson.

The men by the vehicles were dead; the other Nazis were falling back towards the gate, bobbing up over the bridge parapet to snap off shots as they retreated.

"Pitch it up, Lucky," said Urbanski, tossing a grenade to his companion. "Right in the slot."

Heedless of the bullets whirring past, Lucky passed his rifle to Urbanski and pulled the pin on the grenade. He calmly wound up like a pitcher on the brink of a World Series win and then let fly.

The soldiers on the stone bridge looked up and back towards the castle as the grenade arced over their heads, bounced on the floor of the archway and disappeared through the open gate. Panicked shouts echoed from within before a loud bang silenced them.

Dixon's men were pushing onwards too, coming at the bridge through the bullet-pocked vehicles. The position for the Germans was hopeless as they were caught in the crossfire, but Urbanski noted not one of them looked afraid nor attempted to surrender.

S.S., he thought. Never know when to quit.

They were cut down in short order. Mayhew and two others raced across the bridge to secure the gate. They threw in another couple of grenades to make sure of anyone past the archway.

"Quickly now, Sergeant Urbanski!"

Weatherall was at Urbanski's shoulder and his voice suddenly close at hand made the sergeant jump.

"Jesus, are you trying to give me a heart attack?"

"The gate, Sergeant Urbanski." Weatherall took out a pocket watch and frowned. "We must hurry up."

Urbanski kept pace with the agent as he ran across the bridge. "What's so damn pressing about the time?"

"Everything, Sergeant Urbanski," puffed Weatherall. "If we dawdle, our target may escape."

The archway led to a tunnel about twenty yards long, and beyond that was a triangular courtyard with the bulk of the castle rearing up on every side, leaving a patch of star-filled sky above. Burning braziers lit the scene, throwing red light against the walls, ruddy glints bouncing back from tiers of windows.

Urbanski was surprised that their arrival did not herald any further gunfire; the tunnel was filled with corpses but the courtyard was quite empty.

His heart was still racing after the exertions of combat. He checked the doorways and roof, but there was definitely nobody else here.

Except that as he calmed he could hear more voices, muffled and distant.

"The North Tower, Lieutenant Mayhew," insisted Weatherall, flapping his bag towards the round tower at the far end of the courtyard.

"Okay, Mister Weatherall, whatever you say," replied the lieutenant. "Dixon, take seven men and clear out the rooms to the east, Parker same to the West. We might as well go straight acro–"

Mayhew stopped as the door at the base of the north tower opened and a figure appeared, pistol in hand.

"Back!" snapped Urbanski, dragging Weatherall by the arm as the agent stepped out into the courtyard.

A bullet sparked off the wall next to the sergeant and whined down the tunnel.

"Let me go, Sergeant Urbanski!" snarled Weatherall. The small man's vicious tone shocked Urbanski into compliance.

A booming German-accented voice echoed across the courtyard, chanting unintelligible words. Urbanski felt something on his foot and glanced down to see one of the S.S. guards stretching out a blood-stained hand towards his ankle. The man's face was slack, pieces of shrapnel buried into his forehead and cheek.

Mayhew noticed the man too and met Urbanski's panicked gaze with a disbelieving stare of his own.

"No, no, no," Urbanski whispered, pulling his foot away sharply. "No, not again."

———————

18:07, 24ᵗʰ March, 1945

"How long's he been muttering like that?" asked Mayhew from halfway down the basement steps.

The S.S. officer was sat on a rickety chair amongst broken boxes and torn sacking, speaking quietly, without pause. His gaze was fixed on a nondescript point at the centre of the cracked plaster ceiling. Urbanski knew some German – being the son of Poles had some advantages – but he couldn't recognise a word the Nazi was saying.

"Just started, sir," reported Lucky. "Thought I'd better tell you."

"Shut your hole, kraut." Mayhew put a hand on his pistol holster and descended a few more steps. "Save your confessions for the Colonel."

The German stopped for a moment, looked at Mayhew with a sneer and then continued murmuring as he returned his gaze to the same point. The lieutenant undid his holster and took another two steps but the sound of a gunshot from above made everyone jerk with shock.

"What?" Mayhew dashed up the steps, Urbanski close on his heel, Lucky and another paratrooper behind him. "Who the hell is shooting?"

More shots rattled out from across the house.

"It's a counter-attack, Lieutenant!" came a reply from the

remains of the lounge at the front of the house. Ramsey and O'Gara were at the large bay window, their rifles poked through the shattered panes of glass.

"There's near enough seven thousand Brits and nine thousand boys from home in this neck of the woods, there ain't no damn counter-attack."

Moving to the window, Urbanski could see grey shapes moving through the rubble of the buildings. They seemed disorientated as they stumbled over the broken bricks and tiles but they were definitely Germans. Looking to the right he could see more converging from where the machine gun nest had been.

As he looked back across the street, the sergeant saw an enemy soldier staggering from the ruins opposite. Shots rang out from above and the German jerked left and right, feet scraping in the dust and stones.

The man kept walking.

"What the hell?" Urbanski stepped up next to Ramsey and fired a burst from his Thompson. At this range, just twenty yards, he couldn't miss. The bullets hit the soldier square in the chest, knocking him backwards.

"See, that's how..." Urbanski's words trailed off as the German continued shuffling towards the house.

A shout from the rear of the building and a crash of glass drew everyone's attention away from the window.

"Check it out, Banksy," ordered Mayhew as he sighted with his pistol through the window.

The sergeant gave Lucky a tap on the shoulder and the two of them set off down the hallway towards the kitchen and parlour; more shots and yells rang out ahead of them.

In the kitchen three paratroopers were at the door, wrestling with a handful of Germans, another two were firing point-blank into another at the window.

The enemy soldiers bore obvious wounds – one had half of his face missing, another waved a stump of an arm as he tried to claw his way through the window – their uniforms hanging in rags to expose bullet holes and shrapnel wounds on limbs and bodies.

There was no way possible they could still be alive.

Even as he tried to come to terms with this terrifying fact, Urbanski heard thuds from the stairs. He left Lucky to help out in the kitchen and headed back to the hallway.

His legs almost buckled and his stomach lurched as he came to the foot of the stairs.

Halfway down was the soldier Urbanski had shot earlier. His chest was a pulsing open wound. His splinter-pierced, burnt face twisted in a grotesque manner as a wordless moan emanated from blistered lips.

Urbanski recovered his wits just as the German was within reach of him. Recoiling from the dead soldier's grasp, the sergeant opened fire, drilling bullets into the apparition bearing down upon him. He kept backing away until he came against the front door, finger squeezing the trigger until his wild hail of fire ended with a loud click of an empty magazine.

The soldier was a bloody, ragged mess at the foot of the stairs. It twitched and raised its head. A bloodshot eye regarded Urbanski with a cold, lifeless stare and a hand coated in dried blood reached out jerkily.

A loud crash from the lounge and a shout from Mayhew announced the arrival of the enemy at the bay window. Ramsey backed out of the room into the hall, blood spitting from a gash in his neck. The paratrooper collapsed to the floor, still firing his rifle as a grey-clad soldier lurched after him.

A deafening, blinding burst of sound and muzzle flare filled the hallway and the German looming over Ramsey was flung back through the door.

At the kitchen entrance stood Lucky, a Browning Automatic Rifle in his hands, gun smoke streaming from its muzzle.

"Holy shit, Sergeant. What the hell is going on?"

The remains of the soldier at the bottom of the stairs was slowly crawling towards Urbanski. The sergeant reloaded without conscious thought, mind whirling at what had happened. Skin crawling, he let loose another burst of fire, obliterating the head of the German at his feet. The enemy soldier finally slumped to a standstill.

Mayhew arrived next, retreating quickly from the lounge, pistol discarded, a Garand in his hands in its place.

"Lieutenant, what do we do? What's happening?" Urbanski pleaded. He turned quickly as movement through the glass of the front door drew his attention. Dark shapes were approaching up the steps.

"Hell if I know," the officer replied.

Mayhew fired through the door of the lounge and stepped back. A look of shocked realisation crossed his face and turned towards the basement door.

"Lucky, hold them off. Urbanski, come with me."

The sergeant followed Mayhew back down into the cellar.

The S.S. officer sat where he had been left, still whispering, hands twitching in his lap.

"Shut up!" yelled Mayhew, pointing his rifle at the enemy officer. "Shut the hell up, right now!"

The Nazi did not stop, but turned his gaze on the two Americans. His eyes shone as if flecks of ice were buried within them.

"Can't hold them!" came Lucky's warning from above. The paratrooper stumbled down onto the steps and slammed the door.

"Stop it, whatever it is you're doing!" Mayhew tossed aside his rifle and grabbed the Nazi by the lapels of his jacket and shook him. "Shut up!"

"Shut up!" echoed Urbanski, eyes flicking in fear between the whispering Nazi and the door at the top of the basement steps.

A dreadful thudding started at the basement door, accompanied by the scratch of fingernails on wood.

Urbanski acted out of pure terror.

With a panicked shriek, he shouldered Mayhew aside, thrust the muzzle of his Thompson into the face of the prisoner and pulled the trigger.

Pieces of skull and brain splattered against the bare cellar wall.

Panting, Urbanski fired again, and again, riddling the Nazi's body with bullets.

There were thumps above; the sound of bodies falling.

"Enough," Mayhew said quietly, laying a hand on Urbanski's shoulder. The sergeant spun around and almost fired at the lieutenant, a mad look in his eyes.

"Sergeant!" the sharpness in Mayhew's tone was matched by the sting of a back-handed slap.

Snapped out of his mania, Urbanski let the submachine gun drop from his numb fingers as he fell to his knees.

It took several minutes for Urbanski to recover; minutes characterised by intermittent sobs and periods of dumb catatonia. Eventually some semblance of sanity reasserted itself and the sergeant allowed Lucky to help him to his feet.

"What the hell are we going to say happened here?" Urbanski asked, looking at the pulped remains of the Nazi officer.

"Nothing, Sergeant." Mayhew shook his head in disbelief. "Nothing happened here. Our prisoner was killed whilst attempting to escape during an enemy counter-attack. That's what my report will say."

"But..." Urbanski waved his arms as he flailed for the right words, trying to encompass everything that had happened over the last few minutes. "What about...? And the..."

"Who would we tell, Banksy?" asked Mayhew. "We got a bunch of shot-up Germans and a load of dead paratroopers. Nothing else. Who would believe us?"

23:49, 30th April, 1948

The courtyard was filled with the flare and din of guns. Urbanski felt cold, numbed to the horror around him. It was as if having confronted the dead before it no longer shocked him. That was not to say he was anything less than utterly terrified, but unlike before this time a kernel of rational, chilling sanity kept him from being overwhelmed by the experience.

Others were not so fortunate. Ryan was hiding in a doorway, gibbering manically, banging his head back against the wall. Simmons was crouched over a corpse, repeatedly punching his fists into the mess of its face, his hands bloodied and broken. A handful of others had simply fled at the first moments of the dead coming back.

Weatherall sheltered behind Mayhew, who was doing his best to coordinate a defence against the mass of Nazis shambling up through the gate corridor. At first Urbanski thought the agent from Washington had lost his mind – he was murmuring and muttering to himself.

Glancing over his shoulder, the sergeant saw that this was not the case. Weatherall was crouched by the wall, his notebook open on the ground in front of him. He was chanting, and though the words were in English, their rhythm and tone reminded Urbanski of the S.S. officer's invocations.

"A well-sheltered spark of becoming fixed in matter, and thus time and measure acknowledge the light of creation... and so develops the rhythm of life by cause-effect. The cause once more rhythmically born as an effect... And so hides creative rule in the Ryta-rule and spirit and energy work as a soul aware of matter."

Urbanski didn't have the first clue what Weatherall was talking about but the agent's words seemed to be having an effect. The corpse-soldiers jerked and swayed, moving even more awkwardly than before. The ice-light that glimmered in their eyes dimmed and their stumbling became without purpose as they bumped into each other, fell to their knees and clawed at the brick of the walls.

"It's working!" gasped Mayhew. The lieutenant looked back at Weatherall, whose face was now slicked with sweat as he continued to recite from his notes, eyes flicking left and right as he slowly turned the pages.

Weatherall thrust a finger towards the door of the North Tower but did not break his concentration or the flow of words. His features became more waxen by the second; the colour drained from his face and his lips and fingers trembled with effort.

"...from three grew four, primal-fire out of turning, so that Gotos' Al might be completed at the innermost levels in the Fyrog..."

"I don't know how long he can keep that up, Lieutenant,"

said Urbanski. He started towards the North Tower. "Best move now."

Mayhew glanced around and signalled for Lucky and a few others to follow. They ran across the courtyard, dodging between the outstretched hands of the confused dead.

The door to the tower was locked, but the wooden frame gave way to solid kicks.

Urbanski went in first and found himself in a large circular hall, the vaulted ceiling held aloft by eight wide pillars. The floor was laid with grey-white marble and at its centre was a round pattern inlaid in green.

Eight figures stood in a circle, one before each pillar, clad in S.S. uniforms with hooded capes of black over them. Each held out a silver dagger in their right hand like a Nazi salute, their lefts raised in clenched fists to their chests, death's heads rings glinting in the pale light that suffused the room.

They seemed oblivious to the entry of the paratroopers. Their sonorous chanting, in the same semi-German tongue Urbanski had heard before, echoed around the hall.

At the heart of the central geometric pattern burned a cold blue flame, which pulsed and dimmed in time with the chant. There was a figure within the unnatural fire, silhouetted but indistinct. It too had its right fist raised, elbow cocked.

A snarl and footsteps warned Urbanski of attack.

He turned just in time to bring up his Thompson to deflect a knife aimed at his throat. The S.S. officer that had appeared at the door previously slashed again at the sergeant's throat.

Lucky arrived, clubbing the officer to the ground in a welter of blows. The Nazi's head cracked against the marble and a pool of blood spread quickly over the stone.

There was no hesitation in Urbanski this time.

He turned his Thompson on the cloaked figures and opened fire, gunning down the closest two with a long burst. Inhuman screeches rang around the hall as Mayhew and the others cut down the rest with a concerted fusillade.

The unnatural flame guttered and died. A plaintive wail issued from the ragged figure that was left standing there. The person took a shaky step liked a crooked marionette and then pitched forward onto its face and lay still.

Mayhew ordered some of the men to spread out and check the rest of the tower while he and Urbanski approached the body at the centre of the hall.

"Well done, gentlemen," said Weatherall from the doorway. The agent seemed years older, his face etched with age and fatigue. He had his notebook under his arm and steadied himself against as he looked at the body of a cloaked Nazi. "We arrived just in time."

"In time for what?" asked Mayhew.

"To stop this, of course, Lieutenant Mayhew," said Weatherall. "It won't be the last time they try, I'm sure of it, but the Fourth Reich has been set back by our intervention here. There will be other attempts, to bring back more of their kind. They went to great effort to lay the path to follow, after all."

"But what did we stop?" Urbanski turned over the burned figure lying in middle of the circle at the room's centre.

The man was of average height, exposed flesh burnt in places down to the bone. Most of the skin had slewed away and there was no hair left on the body. There was a distinctive bullet hole in the man's right temple.

There was something familiar about him that Urbanski couldn't quite place for a moment. And then realisation came.

"It can't be?" he said as he stood up, incredulous.

"Yes, Sergeant Urbanski." Weatherall crossed the hall and laid a hand on Urbanski's arm. "We've just prevented the unholy return of the Secret King himself. Adolf Hitler. His presence would have been a considerable boost to the Nazi resurrectionists. We have done a good thing today, be proud gentlemen."

Mayhew and Urbanski exchanged a glance. The lieutenant shook his head wryly.

"Nothing to report, I take it?" Urbanski said to Weatherall. "Just a group of war criminals killed whilst resisting arrest?"

"You are very smart. Nothing unusual to report at all, Sergeant. Nothing at all."

JAMIE MASON

Jamie Mason is a Canadian sci-fi/fantasy writer whose short fiction has appeared in Abyss & Apex, On Spec, the Canadian Science Fiction Review and been anthologized in *Dead North* and *Fractured: Tales Of The Canadian Post Apocalypse* (Exile Editions, Nov 2014). His novel *Echo* was published in June 2011 and his post-apocalyptic novel *The Book Of Ashes* is forthcoming from Permuted Press. Learn more at www.jamiescribbles.com

ETERNAL REICH

BY JAMIE MASON

Like most old villains who have escaped justice, I nurse secret guilt. Like many who worked in the concentration camps, I live in fear that someday a face from the past will reappear. The irony that my physician at this rest home is a Jew is not lost on me. He suspects nothing of my prior life and is as diligent in his attentions to me as he is kind. We have different reasons for not raising history. His is ignorance - mine, secrecy. In this we are each the product of an age.

This place, with its gentle regimentation and infinity of pastels, appalls me. A warehouse for the old. I consume the bland food and television and endure the equally bland company - spoiled octogenarians edging toward death on a carpet of pharmaceuticals. I'm the only one here who smokes. And, to my knowledge, the only one who wakes terrified by nightmares that are products not of imagination but memory.

I smelled jasmine today and was again a young intern on that afternoon in 1941 when Doctor Hofmann first brought me to the blockhouse containing the six coffins.

Coffins were common enough in Ravensbrück. But these were exceptional for their quality and craftsmanship – a far cry from the pine boxes used to inter deceased menials and prisoners until we abandoned the practice in favour of mass graves. The six caskets rested on fresh-cut sawhorses in the gloom of their block-walled enclosure. The place was otherwise unfurnished, save for a life-sized crucifix at one end. I examined this strange ornament with interest. At points where the figure would have been secured by wrists, ankles and neck were loops of barbed wire. I recall Hofmann's making some jest about Christ's questionable parentage. Still young enough to be unsettled by blasphemy, but eager for his approval, I answered with a watery smile. Hofmann was the S.S. doctor in charge of "special experiments" at the camp. His support was fundamental to advancement.

He was crisp and to the point. I had been selected to document this important experiment because of my unique diligence and loyalty. The room itself was guarded 'round the clock by members of an elite team of *Leibstandarte S.S. Adolf Hitler*, entry being restricted to us and one other whom Hofmann said would arrive shortly. I was to be promoted, re-assigned permanently to the doctor's staff and moved to private quarters. Under no circumstances, Hofmann stressed, was I to fraternize with former colleagues or discuss my work in the blockhouse with anyone. The penalty should I do so? His eyes wandered to the cross. I might have reacted with a burst of youthful indignation had I not been so terrified by the doctor's calm - almost fond – gaze toward the instrument.

The door opened.

Much has been written about the experience of meeting Reinhard Heydrich. S.S.-*Obergruppenführer* and head of the Reich Security office, mostly by people who never did. The menace the man conveyed with his artic gaze and eerie stillness is impossible to exaggerate. Heydrich was a confidante of Hitler himself, and it was at his urging that the S.S. undertook Final Solution of the Jewish Problem, constructing its archipelago of death camps across the Reich. I was seized by an uncontrollable fit of trembling in Heydrich's presence – an instinctual clutch of deep-rooted fear, like a man stumbling upon a wolf in the forest.

Heydrich dismissed me with a glance. Addressing Hofmann exclusively, he said that data from the current trials was imperative. A favourable outcome was crucial so the General Staff would authorize deployment of what Heydrich termed "the assets" to Czechoslovakia, where they were desperately needed. He would be in Berlin, awaiting Hofmann's memo with interest. With that – and without a second glance my way – Heydrich left. The palpable sense of menace in that room, with its six coffins and macabre instrument of torture, abated measurably. I recognized that I had just been in the presence of a man both powerfully brilliant and completely psychotic.

I was taken to the administrative offices and introduced to a corporal from the Wehrmacht documentary film office who would instruct me in the use of a hand-held movie camera. I learned fast and enjoyed the technical aspects of this new skill. At the completion of the tutorial, I was given two fine quality German-made Hasselblad 8mm movie cameras and a selection of customized Zeiss lens attachments. I encountered Hofmann in the hallway afterward. He said a desk and chair had been placed in the blockhouse for my use and bid me report there to await further instructions.

I mulled the day's events crossing the deserted exercise yard toward the concrete bunker. An unsmiling S.S. guard unlocked the door. It took a moment for my eyes to adjust to the windowless gloom. When they did, I was shocked to see a man in a dove-grey S.S. uniform standing wreathed in cigarette smoke, his back to me.

I was struck immediately by the jasmine essence permeating his tobacco. Emboldened by recent promotion, I demanded he identify himself at once. His back stiffened when I spoke and he began to turn. It was only then that I realized the lid of one coffin was now open.

I cease my reminiscences and go in search of food. The dormitory wing of the rest home is deserted at this hour of the morning. Only one orderly is on duty in the cafeteria. To my delight, it is Chico, a Puerto Rican man with whom I am simpatico. He brews the extra strong coffee forbidden me by the nurses and we adjourn to the parking lot, smoking together. I ask after his wife and baby daughter and he inquires about my health. Standard banter. My attention is drawn to an unfamiliar black sports car with heavily tinted windows parked below a streetlamp at the edge of the lot.

"Belongs to the new doctor," Chico says. "The one replacing Dr. Kaplan."

I am surprised to learn that Kaplan, my physician, will be retiring at week's end. Chico's expression reveals they hadn't planned on telling me. I ask the name of the new doctor, but Chico does not know. So I shrug, immune to sentimentality. I will learn the name of the new physician with the flashy sports car (- no doubt an aging Lothario with hair implants and a golf tan -) in due time. For now, I am adrift in that sea of ignorance so different from my days as a physician's apprentice at Ravensbrück, when I knew so much and the rest of the world, so little ...

Where was I?

The S.S. man in the blockhouse turned, eyes narrowing as he crossed his arms and studied me. Where Heydrich instilled the fear of a vicious animal, this man (whose insignia designated him an *S.S.-Standartenführer*) exuded a menace so profound that, in his presence, one found oneself suddenly immersed in nightmare - the same paralysis, stilling of the breath and sense of time slowing attended him. *I discovered that I could not move.*

Did we, in our primeval past, ever have a natural predator, the sight of whom struck terror in our hearts? If so, this man – this slender, dark-eyed *Standartenführer* – was surely such a one.

"You have your camera, Herr Doktor?"

The voice: dry, small. I nodded. I was under this man's sway as surely as if he were the Führer himself, and his wishes - though unspoken - were perfectly clear. I was to sit at my desk in the corner and begin filming at once.

Reviewing the silent black and white footage (as I often did in the final hours before the Russians stormed the camp) never failed to leave me horror-struck by the grim spectacle that unfolded.

The lid of another coffin raised and a second man, attired as the first in the dove-grey uniform of the S.S., emerged. He moved to stand beside the *Standartenführer* briefly before the two walked – glided would be more precise – toward the door. Two sharp raps and it was opened, the elite S.S. guard outside handing something to the men.

It was a girl.

Small, slim-hipped, dark eyes wide with fear, she stumbled barefoot into the room to be caught at bicep and elbow by the second S.S. officer. I recognized her as one of the "rabbits" – Polish women selected for use in medical experimentation. Inured to every horror though she must have been, I cannot imagine what terror was writing itself in a wordless scream across her face. The *Standartenführer* closed the door.

They fastened her to the cross: neck, wrists and feet. I continued filming. The nightmare had consumed me. I was invisible. Even to myself.

The remaining four coffins opened one by one and men arose – dark-eyed, slender, graceful men in immaculate S.S. uniforms and polished boots, their insignias glittering. They marshalled before the cross at attention, eyes front, heels together. The *S.S.- Standartenführer* walked calmly up and down the line, inspecting them. Only when he was satisfied each was properly turned out and poised in that unnatural stillness of theirs did he turn to the rabbit on the cross.

I mean – of course - the *girl*.

Swiftly, he struck. Her right arm snapped at the elbow. I heard - but never even saw - the blow. One moment, the girl was stiff against the wood, eyes wide with fear, but silent. The next she was screaming, struggling against her bonds even as they cut her body, limp arm flapping in its bracelet of barbed wire. Then they were upon her.

They swarmed, these guardians of the Fatherland: swarmed and tore and ripped in a frenzy like wild animals. They were *feeding*. The girl was taken apart piece by piece, organ and bone, the flesh peeled from her wriggling, howling form in precise strips. Only when she began to faint was the method to the *Standartenführer's* madness made plain. For each time the rabbit swooned toward the relief of unconsciousness, someone would yank at her broken arm and she would awake in a fresh burst of screaming. And the carnage would continue. She died a million deaths on that cross, denied the final relief until the last possible moment, when barely her face, skeleton and feet remained. She died in the fury of the final onslaught, in crashing waves of blood.

Strange that she should find rest amid that cruel frenzy. Stranger still that, despite the carnage, not one of the attackers' uniforms was soiled by a single drop of blood.

She died with a final spasm. The men returned to stand in ranks. A brief, silent dismissal from the *Standartenführer* sent them back toward their coffins, into which each lowered himself with military precision, pulling the lid shut behind him. The *Standartenführer* was the last in, pausing to survey the room with a final glance as if a battlefield from which his men, now safe in their transport and anxious to be gone, awaited their commander. The 8mm film captured the final moments of this tableau when he paused to gaze at me before retreating to his coffin ...

I am haunted, even now, by what I saw in those eyes.

We're celebrating a birthday in the rest home. Mr. Kopek, a Romanian, turns 94 today. After lunch, we don paper hats and loiter around the edges of the common room, awaiting cake while a chorus of nurses warbles "Happy Birthday" to a wizened creature in a wheelchair. I slip away, fetch cigarettes and limp to the parking lot. Chico is there. We take up our customary positions either side of the sand-filled bucket by the loading dock and smoke.

The smell of jasmine is strong in my nostrils. Odd, as it is out of season. The weight of my memories pressing down on me is no doubt to blame. I am enshrouded in the scent, eyes watering, too distracted to reply even when Chico mentions the new doctor is a smoker. I force air from my lungs as I return indoors, willing myself to be rid of it: the stench of jasmine - eternally tainted for me with recollections of violent death.

More singing from the common area. The sound chases me back into my memories and I am reminded of another party from which I once sought refuge ...

Summer, 1942. I was drinking heavily – a by-product of my work in the blockhouse, where uneventful days would accumulate until suddenly the lid of the furthest coffin would raise and the *S.S. Standartenführer*, whose name was Hecht, emerge. His advent always signalled a coming carnage. He would smoke one of those noxious cigarettes before going to the door to admit that day's victim. Sometimes it was a fully-grown woman, sometimes a child who was scheduled to be crucified and butchered as the Polish girl had been. Sometimes the *Standartenführer's* group attacked en masse and sometimes varied routine by attacking one at a time. What never changed was the grisly outcome, nor my silent complicity as I sat filming, awash in hellish torment.

Why did these executions upset me so? I was – and remain – an ardent Nazi, believer in the doctrine of racial purity and convinced of the need for judicious extermination of inferiors. As a physician, I attended numerous executions. And yet the sadistic killings in the blockhouse unsettled me with their artistic cruelty. There was something hauntingly inhuman about them. I began taking refuge at a café in the village.

One night in June, I arrived to find a party in progress. I fled to a back room with three tables and ordered a bottle of red wine, which I proceeded to consume at alarming speed. I ordered a second and, before it arrived, paid a visit to the lavatory.

I was washing up when the sad-eyed man in the trenchcoat found me. His name, he said, was unimportant. What mattered was whom he represented – an echelon of Soviet military intelligence known as the NKVD. He had traveled into Germany at considerable personal risk to contact me.

"We know you are keeping Colonel Hecht and his henchmen at Ravensbrück," he said in perfectly accented German – a Prussian intonation, to be exact. His linguistic pedigree was undeniably aryan; his handlers had been thorough.

"What has this to do with me?" I demanded.

He smiled wearily. "My superiors want Hecht dead."

The wine, the burden of my grisly work and these outrageous words combined to strike me dumb. I swallowed thickly. As if sensing hesitation, the man in the trench-coat bid me consider his words carefully, promising he would be in touch, then turning to go. Upon reaching the door, he paused to mention that – should

I doubt the gravity of our meeting – he was authorized to inform me that an important assassination had been carried out earlier that day in Prague. It would, he assured me, become common knowledge very shortly.

He left without another word.

I ran my hands under the faucet, trembling, too befuddled to recognize - until drying them - that I was repeating an action I'd already performed. Fighting to clear my head of everything, I craved more wine and the oblivion it would bring. Stepping out of the bathroom into the now silent restaurant, I saw a waiter standing by the kitchen door. He reached out to turn up the radio to which everyone was listening.

The broadcast announced the assassination of Reinhard Heydrich in Prague earlier that day.

Hofmann summoned me to his office the next morning. The future of the experiment, he said, was now uncertain. The assassination of Heydrich - who had recently been appointed military governor of Czechoslovakia - unsettled many things, not least of which was the fate of the six coffins in the blockhouse. Progress had stalled on the Russian front, prompting a re-evaluation of priorities at all levels. Pet projects of recently deceased military governors were decidedly low on that particular list. Hofmann assumed a decision on the future of the "assets" would be forthcoming but, until then, Colonel Hecht and his men would have to be accommodated.

"Keep them quiet," Hofmann instructed, "until I figure out what to do with them."

I dragged myself to the blockhouse, hoping for an uneventful day. The first few hours were exactly as I had wished. Having grown accustomed to sitting alone at a desk in a cold room with only the dead for company, I calmly read the newspapers until lunch. Then I took up my thermos and packet of sandwiches. I no sooner unwrapped the first from its wax paper than a stirring arose and the lid of Hecht's coffin trembled. My arm froze in the act of lifting a sandwich to my mouth.

With an anguished groan, the coffin lid gave way to stand on its hinges. Hecht sat upright, turning to fix me with that hypnotic glare of his. I wondered: *does he know about Heydrich*? As if sensing the question, the Colonel allowed his eyes to linger on me for a minute before bringing slim hands to the coffin's edge and vaulting, with eerie grace, to the floor. The sound of boot heels striking concrete rang in the cold air.

Hecht extracted his lighter and silver cigarette case and carefully lit one of his jasmine-tinctured cigarettes. He stood watching me as he smoked, smiling, unspeaking, apparently enjoying my discomfort. Then, cigarette finished, he ground the remains under his boot and marched to the door, rapping on it sharply twice.

There was no answer.

Hecht stood with shoulders hunched, appearing to marshal his patience before knocking a second time. Again, there was no response. My heart leapt. Had the *Leibstandarte* been instructed to cease cooperating with him? The Colonel raised his fist to rap again, then seemed to change his mind. He turned slowly. His gaze, terrible in its power, reached out and closed around me like a fist.

His meaning was perfectly clear.

I closed my eyes.

Thus it was that I grew ever more complicit in the murders committed by the otherworldly Colonel Hecht and his men. For, in the absence of cooperation from the S.S., I became the one who procured their victims. To do otherwise would have displeased Hofmann (and, no doubt, led to my immediate placement on the cross by Hecht in substitution for any missing "rabbits").

A coward's rationale if ever there was one.

"We will be working together more closely now, ja?" Hecht whispered in his dry little voice, handing me a slip of paper.

I would unfold these slips to find written on them the particulars of the desired victim (for instance, one might say: "mature female, post-menopausal, Jew"). I began regularly crossing the exercise yard to the gate that led into the main camp. There, with the assistance of a guard, I located individuals meeting the requirements and brought them to the blockhouse, handing the victims over to Hecht and his men. Then I returned to my desk to load a camera with film and document the ensuing carnage.

This ritual repeated itself time and again throughout the summer and into the autumn of 1942. The slips of paper inked by Hecht's precise hand were stored in the top right-hand drawer of my desk: "young female, pubescent, Gypsy"; "mature female, fertile, Jew"; "infant, male." The stack of papers grew as did my canisters of developed film, returned in their fireproof cases from the Gestapo processing lab in Berlin. Also growing were my anguish, dependence on alcohol and sedatives and chronic nightmares that led to a morbid insomnia. I was the walking dead.

I made the decision to kill Hecht in October.

Sad eyes smiled at me across a schooner of beer. The NKVD man assured me he could supply weapons and expertise. I refused them, along with any offer of asylum inside the Soviet Union. No place on Earth could provide sanctuary from my memories. And I had at my disposal what weapons I needed. All I required from him was a single forged document. Two weeks later, it was supplied.

My appearance the next morning at the blockhouse with a camp orderly wheeling a fireproof filing cabinet on a handcart raised an eyebrow from the lone guard on duty. I explained in my best official tone there were urgent matters requiring my immediate attention and that he was to admit my assistant and me at once. He complied, but insisted on taking over the handcart for the journey across the threshold. I requested he escort the orderly back to the main camp and then complete a small errand on my behalf that would ensure his absence for several minutes. I closed the door behind him.

The coffins rested silently on their sawhorses.

Working quickly, I unlocked the cabinets and removed the two jerry cans of gasoline secreted there. I soaked the desk, chair and cross and then, beginning in the far corner of the room, proceeded to empty both cans until the floor was awash. Assuring myself the guard had not returned, I stepped to the threshold.

My lighter was in my hand when I saw the lid to Hecht's coffin tremble.

Either him or me ...

I struck the flint and dropped the lighter to the floor.

There was a sputtering pop, as of a bottle coming uncorked. Flame chased soft blue flame across the ocean of gasoline from one corner of the blockhouse to the other. In the seconds between the initial spark and the opening of Hecht's coffin, everything inside the room began shimmering with a soft, luminous glow.

Hecht's fingers curled around the edge of the lid and began pressing upward, grey-clad arm straightening as it bore the casket's weight. I saw the edge of Hecht's face materialize from the shadows within, a startled expression beginning to form there.

With a roar, the ocean of gasoline on the floor ignited, sheets of orange flame vaulting from object to object in the room like burning eagles. Hecht sat bolt upright, rage plain in his eyes as the cross exploded in a meteoric blaze. His fingers scrabbled at the edge of the coffin seeking purchase only to be driven back by a wave of flame. An instant later his hand and sleeve caught fire and he lifted it to his face, eyes widening as the flesh melted from his bones.

"Burn," I whispered. "Burn you *verdamte* vampire ..."

The inferno crested, catching the satin lining of Hecht's coffin. His hair caught, skull suddenly engulfed in a sheet of flame. Then the other coffins. There came the hiss of flesh burning followed by the hideous crack as coffin wood split. I was amazed at the sheer speed of the flames, the swiftness in which the temperature in the blockhouse rose and the bodies and coffins burned. I could see the dim outlines of bones writhing inside as they became translucent in the instant before disintegration. I closed the door.

The resulting firestorm blew off the roof of the blockhouse.

By the time Hofmann reached my side demanding an explanation, I had the forged document ready for him.

S.S. General Order 23-12-1013
Immediate destruction of all assets
of Project Hydra stored at Ravensbrück.
Signed,
Heinrich Himmler
Reichsführer, S.S.

I heard a howl and looked up, imagining I saw the twisted black form of a disembodied figure surging upward on the smoke, fleeing earth for the cold darkness of space ...

A hand falls to my shoulder.

Chico

"When you're done writing, the new doctor wants to see you," he says.

I grunt, close my notebook and stand.

"He's German, like you. You'll get to speak in your own language again."

"And he smokes?"

Chico laughs. "Yes. Awful jasmine-scented cigarettes. I met him by the ashtray outside." He holds the door open for me. "He says his name is Hecht."

ALEX HELM

Alex Helm has always had an interest in the fantastical, the futuristic and the bizarre and has frequently been accused of having her head in the clouds. A keen live action roleplayer, historical re-enactor and cosplayer, Alex likes nothing more than spending a weekend dressed up in heavy armour and running around outdoors taking part in battles and pretending to be someone far more interesting (and with more interesting problems).

She started writing fiction while in primary school and dabbled in the occasional story ever since. It's perhaps only in the last three years or so that she really started to focus on making a go of getting published. So far it seems to be going quite well!

She qualified with degrees in materials engineering and computer science, but her history has featured little of either. Previous work experiences have included being a nuclear safety engineer, a World of Warcraft gamemaster, a lawyer (briefly), a database admin and a rocket scientist.

Alex is a self-confessed crazy cat lady, and lives to serve her feline overlords. On the whole, she prefers cats to people, mainly because when the cats are being really annoying, she can chuck them outside... She also has the sweetest tooth on the planet and would happily sell her soul for chocolate (although it is speculated that she already has).

RED WAS THE NIGHT

BY ALEX HELM

Y*ou can escape, but you will never leave.* That's what the old colonel had said, although the meaning of his cryptic words had been lost on me at the time. This was Oflag-IV-C at Colditz Castle, the most notorious prisoner-of-war camp in the whole of Nazi Germany. It was a thousand or so square yards of malevolent stone walls on a hilltop, designed to keep the most 'incorrigible' Allied prisoners locked away until Germany emerged victorious at the end of the war. Of course, the 'fact' of Germany's impending victory was about as accurate as its belief that nobody ever escaped from Colditz. That is to say, not at all.

I am Flight-Lieutenant Terry Easton, a Spitfire pilot from Great Britain. Not a particularly good pilot, it must be said – I was shot down over France during my second mission. Having found myself in a field with nothing but a spent parachute and a ration pack, I was promptly captured by the Nazis and incarcerated in the nearest POW camp. Security was light, and it didn't take me long to come up with a plan to escape. A few cut wire-fences later I was out and about enjoying my freedom. I was re-captured twice, but managed to get away both times. Who would have thought that a childhood injury in the form of a dislocated thumb could be so useful? Being able to pop it in and out ever since has proved to be highly effective in escaping from handcuffs. Harry Houdini, eat your heart out.

My repeated escapes earned me the colourful label of 'incorrigible', and after being captured for the third time, they finally figured out how I was doing it. As my prize, I was carted off to Colditz. It was here that the Nazis sent all those other Allied officers who refused to sit out the war on their backsides and instead created further annoyances for the Germans by escaping.

This plan was somewhat short sighted. What the Nazis had hoped to achieve by locking up the most prolific escapees in one place and giving them nothing to do was beyond me. Suffice to say the greatest minds in escapology came together and numerous plans were formed and executed. The castle became riddled with tunnels.

After spending two years assisting in multiple escape plans, it was my turn to make a break for it. I left with three other men through a tunnel that had taken years to dig. So many bunk bed boards had been used to prop it up that some bunks only had three boards left. The sounds of men on upper beds falling through the gaps onto the lower ones became common.

It took a good hour for us to wriggle through the tunnel and drop into the sewers. This was hardly the most pleasant experience of my life, but what it lacked in rose-fragranced luxury, it made up in pure satisfaction. We climbed up through a manhole and breathed in the scent of freedom. It smelt of dung, but that may have just been our clothes.

We had decided in advance that we were going to split up as soon as we were out, in order to evade detection and to improve the chances of at least one of us making it home. As a result I quickly found myself alone. There I was, a non-German-speaking Englishman in Nazi Germany, covered in shit and missing any form of documents. The clothing problem was easy to solve – the age-old trick of nicking some clean clothing from a washing line worked fine. The lack of documents was a bigger problem. I'd just have to use that famous British wit and ingenuity instead. What could possibly go wrong? I'd be home in no time!

I lasted two days on the run. I headed away from Colditz Castle by stowing away on a freight train for a couple of hours. I even managed to avoid a patrol by hanging from the bogies underneath the carriage. When the train came to a halt and showed no signs of moving further, I scurried off into the countryside. I think I was perhaps some fifty miles from Colditz.

At this point, laying low seemed like the best thing to do, as no doubt our escape had been discovered by now. I spent the next two days in the woods, stealing food and water whenever I could. I even survived a close encounter with a furious broom-wielding

RED WAS THE NIGHT

German housewife by jumping off the edge of a bridge into the river.

It's a shame that I wasn't some kind of machine, capable of keeping going until hitting France and then England. The need to sleep presented the biggest risk, but there were also all of the concerns of eating and, well, doing one's business. It was the latter that sadly resulted in my downfall. There I was, crouched under a bush with my trousers around my ankles, when I was suddenly jumped by a huge black dog. It turned out that the dog just wanted to be friendly. Sadly, the farmers who owned him were less forthcoming. It didn't take them long to figure out that I was an escaped POW and I was smacked over the head with a stick, and the next thing I knew I was waking up in a police cell.

The local police officer was named Wertz. He didn't speak a word of English, and I knew a grand total of about a dozen words of German, picked up from my time at Colditz. Despite the communication issue and the misfortune of my circumstance, he was polite and friendly and even brought cups of tea to my cell. It was delicious English tea that, judging by the cheeky smile on his face, had been somehow illicitly obtained. I decided to sit back and enjoy his hospitality for I knew what was going to be coming next. Although I had yet to encounter them myself, there had been multiple accounts of the Gestapo from the chaps in Colditz. What they had said sounded horrific and in many cases unbelievable. If half of it was true, the Allied authorities back home had no idea what was going on here.

Sure enough, the following day, Wertz and his staff began to look nervous, muttering to themselves and glancing through the bars at me. I didn't need to know any German to recognise the word 'Gestapo', or to pick up the name they mentioned – Gotthardt. *Kriminalkommissar* Gotthardt. The name was not unknown to me – Gotthardt had been mentioned multiple times back in Colditz, and what I had heard wasn't good. The man had been described as a monster in multiple accounts, although no one in the camp had actually met him; they had only heard the screams of those who did. Even though my cell was relatively warm, I shuddered.

A few hours later, I heard the sound of a vehicle pulling up outside the police station, and my friendly host scurried out to meet the new arrivals. Wertz returned some minutes later with four men. Three of them were dressed in grey uniforms bearing the sinister insignia of the S.S., the black right-side collar patch clearly marking them as members of the Gestapo, whilst the fourth, the leader, was in plain clothes – a simple but well-tailored white linen suit, with a black fedora. Dark sunglasses covered his eyes, and what I could see of his face was sallow and sickly. This could only be Herr Gotthardt of the Gestapo.

Gotthardt stalked across the room towards the bars of my cell, his smart patent black leather shoes clacking against the ceramic tiled floor. The Gestapo men followed him with Wertz trailing nervously behind. They stopped a foot or so from the bars and stared at me silently through his sunglasses for a good minute or so at least.

"Um, hello?" I said eventually, anything to break that awkward silence. "Are you bringing more tea? You know we English love our tea."

Gotthardt didn't move or speak. I tipped my head slightly trying to get a feel for him, and I suddenly found myself feeling extremely glad that I couldn't see through his sunglasses. My eyes widened in panic as I gasped and took a step back, wanting nothing more than to get as far away from him as possible, preferably to the other side of the world. My skin grew clammy and I felt my heart pounding. I began taking deeper breaths, and I could feel every nerve in my body twitching in fear. Never in my life had I felt this kind of primeval dread. Even the intense terror of being shot down out of the sky by an enemy plane hadn't scared me remotely this much.

The man didn't move. With his pallid flesh and motionless demeanour, he could have been a statue carved from marble. An extremely terrifying statue that I knew would haunt my nightmares for the rest of my life. I found myself thanking God above that this time was likely to be very short indeed, even my natural fear of death paled into insignificance compared to the terror he inspired.

"You think you are a funny man, Herr Easton," said Gotthardt, finally breaking his silence and speaking in perfectly pronounced yet accented English. His voice was as cold as the arctic wind and I felt another shiver run through me.

"Nonsense. I *know* I am a funny man." I don't know why I kept trying to wind him up. Perhaps it was just my way of coping with the hysterical need to run away screaming. "You obviously want me. You even know my name."

"I know much about you, Herr Easton. One could say I know *everything* about you."

"Well good then. You won't need to torture it out of me. I've heard about your Gestapo, *Mister* Gotthardt."

"I'm sure you have," he said and then paused, clearly for effect. "I can tell you now that it's much worse." He spun around on his right foot and nodded to the guards, barking orders at them in German. I didn't need to know the language to get the gist – he was telling them to bring me along.

My cell was unlocked and thick uniformed arms grabbed me and hauled me out, expertly cuffing my hands behind my back. As I was dragged through the doors towards the waiting vehicle outside, I caught one last glance of the friendly Wertz. He looked apologetic and shook his head sadly, and then he was gone.

The vehicle turned out to be an ominously black van. I was shoved into the back and squashed onto a narrow bench between two of the guards. Of Gotthardt, there was no sign – I assume he sat in comfort in the front of the vehicle. Suffice to say the journey passed unpleasantly. I estimated we spent a couple of hours on the move, and by the end of the windowless trip, I felt really quite sick and my cuffed arms were stiff with cramp. The temptation to free myself using my old trick of dislocating my thumb had been tempting, but I resisted. I was in deep trouble and I didn't want to waste the only ace up my sleeve by using it too early. No, I would bide my time and wait for the best moment, hoping that these people hadn't yet obtained my papers from Colditz.

By the time we reached our destination and I was hauled out of the vehicle it was beginning to get dark. In the shadowy pale dusk, I caught a glimpse of the horizon. The silhouette of a familiar squat shape loomed across the area – Colditz Castle. It seemed I had returned to the town at the base of the hill.

The building that we were heading into was presumably the office for the Gestapo in this region. It was a squat concrete structure, two stories high with small windows, sprawling in a horseshoe shape around three sides of the courtyard we had pulled into. Glancing down, I caught glimpses of faded childish chalk patterns on the ground of the courtyard, and I realised that this place must once have been a school. As I was shoved inside, I shivered and not just from the chill in the breeze. The whole place resonated with a sense of foreboding and innocence lost. Until today, I had never really believed in the concept of 'evil' in the biblical sense. I had always thought that people, even the Nazis, were just people. Gotthardt and this place were causing me to seriously rethink that.

We walked through a series of narrow corridors. Grim bulletin boards and Nazi flags had been hung over the walls, but I still caught glimpses of colour and life underneath, faded and lost. Perhaps it was some metaphor for the state of my life right now. I was sure I could hear screams and howls of fright and agony from deep within these walls, but it could just have been my imagination playing games. Despite the sense of evil hanging over this place, it seemed to be nothing more than administrative in nature.

We halted in front of a plain door and one of the guards brought out a ring of keys. He unlocked the door with a rattle and pushed it open. I had inadvertently held my breath at the horrific sight that was sure to greet me inside, but it turned out to be nothing more than a small windowless room with institutional cream walls and a complete lack of bloodstains. The only furniture was a small metal table and two matching chairs. An electric light bulb hung from a short cable from the ceiling. I was marched inside and made to sit on one of the chairs. My cramped arms screamed in agony, but no one removed the cuffs. One of the guards remained by the door to keep an eye on me and the other left, closing and locking the door behind him.

I sat and waited. What else could I do? A tense few minutes

passed before I glanced up at my guard. "Any chance of some water?" I asked, hoping to get him to leave so that I could attempt an escape, but he just ignored me. I sighed and waited for my fate.

I honestly don't know how much time passed in that little room. It could have been hours, or it could just have been minutes. Somehow, time seemed to stand unnaturally still, not even broken by the intermittent flickering of the light. I began to believe I was somehow going insane. No doubt this environment had been specifically designed to break down a prisoner's defences. I decided I wasn't going to be so easily broken!

"I really could use some water," I said again eventually, this time actually meaning it. My throat had become completely parched during the nervous wait.

The guard turned and unlocked the door, causing my heart to surge with short-lived hope before crushing disappointment came in the form of Herr Gotthardt, who stepped into the room, still wearing his coat, hat and sunglasses. As he walked over to me, I once again felt that sensation of absolute ice-cold terror. There was just something completely unnatural about him. I really couldn't explain it.

The guard left the room at this point, closing but not locking the door behind him. Now there was just me and this demon from my childhood nightmares staring down at me.

This time I didn't allow the tense silence to even begin. I pulled my gaze upwards to meet his. "Are we going to talk, or are you just going to watch me again?" I croaked. "We'll talk," he said, once again speaking in that perfectly pronounced English, heavy with the German accent. He carefully sat down in the other chair and tapped his gloved fingers against the table.

"Well, good," I replied, feeling more and more unnerved. I somehow wished he would just get on with it and shoot me. "What do you want to talk about? You said you already knew everything about me."

"I do," he agreed, his voice lacking any kind of emotion. He didn't sound satisfied or pleased or even bored. He just sounded cold. "But tell me anyway. For the record, so to speak. Name."

"Terence Easton. Terry to my friends. That doesn't include you."

"Age."

"What will happen if I don't tell you?"

"Do you really want to find out?" The chill in his voice made me certain that I didn't.

"Twenty-nine."

"Parents?"

"I barely remember my father. He was a conscript who died in the trenches of France when I was a child. My mother, Julie, brought me up. All of this is in my prison files."

The interrogation, such as it was, progressed. He seemed to want to know everything about me – about my childhood, my jobs, my induction into the Air Force. I answered all of his questions, anything to keep him talking and not hurting me. At last we moved onto my exploits in Colditz and my subsequent escape.

"Why did you escape?"

"Why not?" Despite my terror of him, I leaned forward, partly to peer at him in an attempt to be menacing, and partly to give my hands a little space to try and break free of the handcuffs. The cramp in my arms made the task difficult, but I began to wiggle my thumb, easing it out of the socket, praying that he didn't know this little detail of my life.

"Do you think this is funny?"

I glanced up at him. "Of course. You're a real joker."

"I never joke, Herr Easton."

"Then what do you want? Look, if you are going to torture me, then let's get on with it. I have a nice comfy bunk back at Colditz waiting for me."

He gave a snort. "You won't be returning to Colditz."

"I was afraid you were going to say something like that." The thumb was free, and now it was just matter of squeezing my hand through the cuff, but it was going slowly. I could barely feel my arms anymore thanks to the cramp. "So what it is going to be? Bullet in the brain and an unmarked grave? Body dropped in the canal?"

Gotthardt didn't respond. He just raised one hand and removed his sunglasses, folding them up neatly and placing them gently on the table. Then he gazed at me.

His eyes were completely black. No coloured iris, no white sclera, just pure black. As I looked into those eyes I sensed despair and hatred, a hungering evil that sought to consume me completely. I yelped and jerked violently away from him, causing my chair to topple backwards and cast me sprawling onto the floor. The painful impact caused my hand to rip through the cuff opening. It hurt, but I was free.

Lying in a heap on the floor, I tried to shuffle away as Gotthardt stood up, but my legs were tangled up in the chair. Somehow I managed to keep my arms behind my back, hiding my escape from view. My hand stung with pain and I suspected most of the skin had been scraped away. I winced slightly as I manoeuvred my thumb back into its socket.

"What are you?" I am ashamed to say I squeaked this question out in terror as I stared up at this creature that surely was not human. My next question took even me by surprise. "Are you a demon?"

"Do you believe in demons?" Gotthardt had removed his coat, draping it neatly over the back of his chair. He then took off his hat and placed it on the table next to his glasses. His head was completely hairless, his flesh grey and pallid from his scalp down to his neck. Thick veins rose against his flesh, throbbing and pulsing, and the black eyes were sunken into his sockets. Although he looked like some kind of rotten cadaver, he was anything. I was suddenly reminded of the horror stories my gran had told me as a child of revenants in the night, the dead come back to life, draining the souls of the living to sustain their immortal existence.

"Not before today," I said honestly. I managed to unhook my foot from the chair legs, kicking away at it frantically.

Gotthardt stepped closer. "There are many mysteries in life and death, Herr Easton."

He opened his mouth, revealing a set of unnaturally sharp teeth, pointed like tiny bayonets. I decided not to wait and grabbed the fallen chair, flinging it with all my strength at the advancing monster. It was a feeble throw; my arms still weak from the cramp, but it took him completely by surprise and that's all that was needed. I leapt to my feet and hurled myself towards the door, yanking it open and almost stumbling through the gap into the hallway beyond.

I didn't look back. All I wanted to do was to get out of there, away from Gotthardt – whatever he was. I turned right along the corridor, remembering that as being the direction we had entered from. It seemed obvious to me as I ran along the passageway that if I could retrace the route taken, I should end up back outside in the courtyard.

I could hear footsteps coming after me – sharp regular beats tapping against the wooden floor with German precision. I didn't look back and kept running down the passageway, expecting any moment to be jumped by burly guards. My shoulder knocked into one of the pin boards and it fell to the floor behind me in a cloud of paper notices.

The passageway ended at a junction with another and I hurled around the corner to the left. There were no windows along here, just one closed door upon another. A few turns later and I felt thoroughly disorientated. There had to be a way out of here!

I knew I was lost when I started to head down a staircase. When I had been brought it, we hadn't used any stairs. However, it was either keep going or turn back towards my pursuers. I started to hurry down the narrow stairwell, expecting it to lead into a cellar of some kind. The first flight of stairs ended on a small landing, and the second set gave up any pretence of decoration, the steps becoming just bare concrete. I pushed open the door at the bottom and hurried through it, slamming it shut behind me.

A flickering low-power electric light bulb hanging from an open cable provided the only illumination. I quickly realised that this wasn't a cellar at all; it was some kind of underground bunker, just a square hole in the ground with cement floor, walls and ceiling. The place reeked of damp and something else, something foul. Two passages led out from this entry chamber and I didn't delay, dashing down the nearest one.

Once again I found myself in a maze of passages, lit up by the occasional bulb. The shadows flickered and danced, and more than once I found myself flinching away in surprise as a black figure leaped out at me, only to discover it was my own shadow. I wasn't alone down here though. I could hear orders barked in German, the echoes making it impossible to pinpoint the direction of the source. I knew I couldn't run forever. Perhaps I could hide for long enough for me to be able to double-back past my pursuers and reach the stairs to freedom.

It was perhaps wishful thinking, but lacking any other options, I pulled open one of the doors and ducked inside, carefully closing it behind me. To my relief, I saw that there was a deadbolt on the inside of this door. The bolt was well-oiled and didn't make a noise, so I slid it silently shut. It was only then that I turned around to see where I had ended up.

Bodies.

There were human bodies in here. A pile of them, just dumped in the middle of the room, gleaming in the flickering light. It was then that the stench hit me. My eyes widened and I found myself stepping forward to look more closely.

The bodies seemed to be of a multitude of people, all adults. Most were male but there were a few females. Some were dressed in civilian clothes while others sported a range of Allied military uniforms. A couple of the bodies were wearing German uniforms, those of the Wehrmacht, not the S.S. I could only assume that this was where the victims of the Gestapo ended up – enemies, traitors and those who simply spoke up against the Nazi regime?

Something looked wrong to me; that is even more wrong than a pile of bodies already looked. I took another step closer and peered over the ghastly pile. All of the corpses were withered and shrivelled up, yet I could tell they hadn't been dead for long. They all bore a massive gouge on their face and it looked as if some creature had bitten a huge chunk from each one and drained their very life out. My gran's stories came back to me once again. Revenants, the risen dead who prolong their existence by eating the life force of others. My gran had told me that they existed across Europe, particularly in the centre. She said they were as walking corpses themselves, entirely unnatural and unholy, existing since the dawn of time.

"I see why you earn your reputation, Herr Easton."

The clinical German voice came from behind me, and I spun around in shock. Gotthardt was standing there, once again wearing his white suit, hat and sunglasses. The door that I had firmly locked now stood open behind him.

I glared at him across the room. "What can I say? They sent me to Colditz for a reason. I'm just that good."

"Of course you are." He cast an arm across the room. "But you present a threat."

"To the Third Reich? Like these poor souls? I highly doubt that." I edged slightly to one side.

"The Third Reich is the here and now. But there was a time before and there will be a time afterwards." Gotthardt didn't move. He just stared at me.

I took another sly step sideways. "Is the whole of the Third Reich... like you?"

"No, Herr Easton. We-"

I didn't wait for him to finish. While he began to make his speech, I dashed forward, slightly to one side of him. His head turned as I moved, but he didn't look concerned even as I barged past and shoved him aside to get through the door.

"There is no escape, Herr Easton!" he said in a loud but calm voice as I ran down the passage, away from that room.

My heart was pounding now, and it wasn't just from the running. I pulled open one door after another, looking for a way out of here, but all I found were rooms full of torture equipment. Much of it looked straight out of the medieval ages, whilst others looked far more modern. There were medical benches covered in straps where a prisoner could be butchered alive. Some of the benches were occupied, and desperate eyes gazed at me as I looked in. To my shame, there was nothing I could do to help them. I nodded back apologetically and then left.

In another room, I found racks of weapons. Whether they belonged to the Gestapo or had been confiscated from their victims, I had no idea. I grabbed a rifle from the nearest rack, a standard German infantry weapon. I looked for ammo and found a five round stripper clip on a shelf. I loaded the gun awkwardly. There wasn't often much call for a pilot to use any firearm larger than a pistol and I'd never been comfortable with rifles in the first place.

I then left the room and turned down another passage, almost running into Gotthardt who was just standing there. I yelped in surprise and turned on one foot to run back the other way. It didn't even occur to me to fire the gun I had picked up. I just wanted to get out of there.

"For centuries they called us witches," he said, his voice echoing through the passages. I kept running, turned one direction then another. Each passage I went down, he was standing there.

"They called us demons and monsters. They hunted us." His voice seemed to be coming from all directions now. I found myself standing in a four way intersection, each passage leading off from it looking identical.

"Perhaps they were right," he continued. I could see his shadow at the end of one of the passages, and I turned around to go another way.

"So we became the hunters ourselves."

I spun around frantically. From all four directions loomed a figure in coat and hat, advancing towards me slowly and calmly.

"We became the witch-hunter army, the Spanish Inquisition, the secret policemen... the Gestapo."

I fought with all my will not to just scream in fear as I turned around. The figures approached, each identical. They were all Herr Gotthardt of the Gestapo.

"We take people off the streets – the heretics, the traitors, the rebels and recidivists."

"And you kill them?" I yelled, my voice breaking in terror. "You eat them? Steal their energy?"

"They are the people our rulers no longer want," he said as if that were justification enough, his voice coming from all directions.

I just wanted to curl up into a ball, hiding my face from these nightmares that sought only to consume me. It would be so easy to give in, to let Gotthardt do what he wanted. At least then I wouldn't be afraid any more.

I didn't surrender to the fear. Instead I finally raised my rifle and took aim at one of the Gotthardts. I wasn't much of a shot, having trained as a pilot rather than a soldier, but rifles were the simplest weapons to use. All I needed to do was point and pull the trigger, so I did.

The gun fired with a massive bang that resonated in my ears, and the stock hammered backwards into my shoulder from the recoil. I could see that I had hit. The Gotthardt I had targeted staggered back from the impact. Yet he just shook his head and after a moment to recover his balance he started approaching once more. In my space at the centre of the intersection, I was close to being completely enveloped by these… creatures.

I fired again and twice more. Each time the figure recoiled from the impact of the shot, but did not pause. Realising that I couldn't stay put, I changed tactics and charged towards him, spinning my gun around in my hands to wield it as a club instead. With a feral yell, I smashed the stock into the side of his head and he staggered to one side.

That was all I needed. I hit him again with my improvised club and then barged past him. Once again I was running down these passages for my life.

I twisted and turned as one Gotthardt after another came out of the shadows. They were laughing at me, a long droning laugh that echoed throughout the maze of the bunker. I spun around, whimpering in terror, crying out for help but none came.

At last I saw the staircase leading back up. Panting in fear and from the exertion I threw myself onto the stairs, scrabbling up them on all fours as my hands and feet clawed for grip. Twice I nearly slid back down as I clutched the battered rifle, desperate not to lose my only weapon. I glanced back down the stairs to see Herr Gotthardt standing at the bottom, still wearing his hat and coat.

"They'll never believe you," he said, disturbingly calmly. "We will find you. You had better find a good place to hide because you'll never return to England."

"Wretched demon!" I yelled after him, my voice almost a screech with fear. "I'll tell everyone about this! I'll tell Churchill himself!"

Gotthardt just laughed. As his cackles resonated through my head, I reached the top of the stairs and left him behind, scurrying off through the corridors of the former school. I gripped my rifle, ready to fire my last shot at anyone who blocked my progress, but I didn't see a soul. My head jerked left and right, looking for any sign of movement, any enemy that I could just kill and end this nightmare, but there was none. The whole complex was silent, deserted. It was if it was dead and had been for years.

At last I came to a sturdy door that looked like it led to the outdoors, but it was locked. I tugged at the doorknob, leaving it slick with the sweat from my hands, but it wouldn't budge. I took a few steps back, raised my rifle and aimed at the knob.

With another loud bang, the doorknob exploded. I dropped the now-empty gun and levelled a heavy kick at the door, smashing it open in a cloud of splinters. Outside was the courtyard, the ghostly childhood drawings glinting in the moonlight. I took a moment to breathe in the cold night air and then hurried out.

I ran for dear life. It wasn't like my previous escape when I had been trying to avoid any kind of notice. I just ran blindly, no longer caring who spotted me as long as I was further and further away from that place, away from him. At last, exhaustion overcame me and I stood on the edge of the town, bent over and gasping for breath. My wits began to collect themselves. Gotthardt has been right about one thing – I needed a place to hide. I needed a place with thick walls to protect me from the monsters, a place that even Gotthardt wouldn't expect to find me.

Still panting for breath, I leant my hands against my knees and lifted my head to look across the horizon. My eyes rose up the hill to the desolate fortress on the rock, standing ever guard across the town and beyond. Colditz Castle. Its walls had once been my prison but now they would be my sanctuary.

It took me an hour to retrace the steps of my escape, to head back through the sewers and the crude tunnel we had dug. The castle end of the tunnel had been blocked up by the guards or perhaps by the other prisoners to hide the opening. I dug at the earth with my own fingers, scrabbling away at it with sheer desperation. At last I broke through and pushed the remaining dirt aside, crawling out to lie shivering on the floor. As my wits gradually returned, I realised that the old colonel had been right about Colditz, although perhaps not in the way he had intended. You can escape, but you will never leave.

Thank you for taking the time to read this book.

We hope you enjoyed it.

More stuff available at www.fringeworks.co.uk
Get involved; follow us on Twitter @fringeworks